PERFECT
PAYBACK

BOOK THREE – THE PEPPERMAN MYSTERY SERIES

PERFECT
PAYBACK

BOOK THREE – THE PEPPERMAN MYSTERY SERIES

BILL BRISCOE

Editor: Lori Freeland
Cover Designed by Fiona Jayde Media
Formatting by The Deliberate Page

Available in eBook & Paperback
eBook ISBN: 978-0-9986425-9-8
Paperback ISBN: 979-8-9854280-0-1

http://billbriscoe.com

This book is dedicated to the memory of
Frederick Jules Pepperman III.
Although we never met,
we became acquainted through my stories.
May the memory of this heroic father live on.

CHAPTER 1

June 1999
Bartlesville, Oklahoma

LIGHTNING CRACKED ABOVE THE HOUSE LIKE ICE FRACTURING a frozen pond. Wind whipped the limbs on the sycamore tree back and forth like flimsy straws and ripped the canvas awning that covered the patio. The fabric slapped violently against the metal supports. Torrential rain slammed the patio door, forcing its way under the frame.

The door blew open, and I fought to close it, my six-four, two hundred fifty-pound body almost useless against the gale-like winds. Oklahoma's weather in late spring and early summer was notorious for freakish storms. But this? This was insane!

"Laura," I yelled to my wife. "Check the windows in the boys' rooms." I hoped they'd remembered to close them before leaving for baseball camp, but I had a sinking feeling they hadn't.

A streak of bluish-white light flashed across the kitchen followed by an angry growl of thunder, killing the power and kicking up my heart rate.

The entire house shook, and the roof seemed to explode. Weather sirens broke through the cool rain-soaked air, the ear-splitting roars mimicking the noise from a WWII documentary.

I froze for a second, then screamed over the storm, "Laura, get away from the windows."

Racing up the stairs, I caught my foot on a step and almost fell.

Another lightning blitz followed the first and came with a *boom* that barraged the house again. *Bam, bam, bam.* Hail hit the window at the end of the hall and pounded against the brick exterior.

I barely saw Laura pressed against the wall shaking, legs pulled to her chest, hands cupped over her ears.

Sinking to the floor, I wrapped my arms around her, pulling her tightly next to me, so close her breath warmed my arm where she tucked her head.

Downstairs in the kitchen, glass shattered against the tile floor. The picture window must have given way to the unrelenting assault. And then... the deluge just stopped. The storm moved on, and the sun peered through the windows.

I got up and flipped the light switch. Nothing happened.

Laura still clutched her knees tight against her chest.

"You okay?" I knelt next to her.

She nodded, looking at me with a crooked grin. "I wet my pants." That expression and her frank admission broke the tension.

My laughter echoed against the wall. "I can't wait to tell the triplets when they get back."

She pointed her index finger at me. "Don't even think about it."

I extended my hand. She latched on, and I pulled her off the carpet. "Let's go check the damage."

"Not until I change my pants and clean the carpet." She tugged on her jeans and wiggled.

I shook my head. Only my wife would worry about a small pee stain on a carpet where three boys had tracked more dirt and grime than a Texas cattle drive. You had to love her. And I did. I'd loved her since my first day of high school in 1966.

The damage downstairs wasn't as bad as I'd expected — only one of the two picture windows had been knocked out. While I waited for Laura, I swept up the shards of glass and covered the empty space with a plastic sheet before heading out to the backyard. A huge branch lay sprawled across the roof. I cleared some of the small limbs from the patio and went back inside.

Laura came out of our bedroom, drying her hair with a towel.

"Did you have to shower and wash your hair too?" I couldn't resist.

She squinted, doubled her fist and shook it. "Not another word, buster, or I'll put an end to the night gymnastics for a couple of weeks."

I extended both hands, immediately defeated. "Got it. Let's go check the attic for damage." We each grabbed a flashlight from the hall closet, and I pulled the ladder down from the ceiling and went first.

Laura gave me a good-natured goose — exactly what I'd expected her to do — and I grinned.

But my grin didn't last long. Considering the size of the tree limb sprawled across our roof, I feared the worst. Rubbing a nervous hand across my mouth, I held my breath and shined my light on the rafters.

The splintered glow gave the attic an eerie *Raiders of the Lost Ark* feel, but no structural damage was evident.

I let out my breath and choked on the dust the tree had stirred up.

I glanced across the cluttered space — cardboard boxes, old toys, baby beds, Christmas decorations. "If a fire started here, the house would go up like kindling."

"Uh huh," Laura muttered from across the corner opposite me.

"We *should* get rid of some of this stuff." We'd been in this house fifteen years, but I wasn't ready to give up the memories it held quite yet.

"Jim, come over here." The excitement in Laura's voice carried across the dark space.

I couldn't imagine what had grabbed her attention. Joining her, I skimmed my light across an old wooden chest with a padlock and a tag with the word *Attic* attached to the lock. "I don't know what this is. I'll get the bolt cutters from the garage." I hurried back to the attic, cut the lock, and lifted the lid, skimming my light across paper-thin fabric clinging to the inside of the old chest.

Laura picked up a photo. "Who are these people?"

I took the picture from her. "It could be..." I checked the back. "Yes, it's Dad and his cousin Hans Pepperman."

Laura took the picture. "The year was 1936. It says Patrick, your dad, was ten years old. Why haven't I heard about Hans?"

"Dad never talked much about his cousin." I didn't know anything about Hans. "What else is there?" Curious, I pointed my flashlight inside.

Laura handed me two letters—one from my Grandfather Wilhelm and one from my dad addressed to Hans. Then she unfolded a white sports jacket. The left pocket had a black patch with an eagle and a white swastika. A label inside read, "1936 *Olympische Spiele*." Laura turned to me. "Do you know what these words are?"

Speechless for a moment, I slowly nodded. "Olympic Games."

"Your cousin participated in the 1936 Olympic Games?" Her eyes widened, and admiration spread across her face.

"I guess so." I crouched on one knee. My chest twitched with pride. Why had Dad never told me? I shook my head repeatedly, not able to fully grasp the thought of a Pepperman participating in the Olympics. The joy was exhilarating.

Laura picked up a program that listed times and places of events. Then she carefully lifted a leather binder with a copper clasp and traced her finger over the name *Hans Joachim Pepperman*. "Let's take it downstairs. I want to read it."

We climbed down the attic ladder and went into the living room.

"I'm calling Mom to see if she knows anything about the trunk." Dialing her number, I anxiously waited for her to answer.

Ring. Ring. Ring.

"Hello."

"Hey, Mom. I need your input on something. I found a trunk in our attic, and it's full of things belonging to a Hans Joachim Pepperman. Who is he? Do you know anything about him or how the trunk got in my attic?"

She cleared her throat. "I don't know much because your dad didn't want to talk about him. It seems the trunk was sent from Germany to your Granddad Wilheim just before the war in Europe broke out. They never had any contact with Hans after they received the trunk. Your grandfather assumed he had become a Nazi. In America, it was not good to have Nazi ties, so your grandfather put a lock on the trunk and tagged it for the attic. Frankly, I'd forgotten about it."

I sighed. "That doesn't tell me how it ended up in my attic."

"Don't you remember? When the truck picked up Laura's things to move to Bartlesville, I had the trunk put on the van. It was the day after you and Laura left on your honeymoon. I told you about it. Or at least I thought I did."

"Hmmm. Okay. I don't remember. But right now, that's not important. A major storm caused a mess. Hail broke a window, and a large tree branch fell on the roof. Let's talk later about the trunk. Love you, Mom."

I went to the living room and joined Laura on the couch.

The journal had a distinct smell. I couldn't describe the odor other than old and musty. My pulse quickened. I was holding a piece of Pepperman history in my hands. History I knew nothing about.

Carefully taking the book from me, Laura released the metal clasp and opened the stiff binding. "It's written in German." Her tone was tainted with disappointment.

I chuckled. "Gee, how inconsiderate of Hans to write his journal in his native language."

She slapped my leg with an open hand.

I took the journal. "I studied German in high school and college."

"Okay, Mr. Linguist, I know you can swear in German. I've heard some words spill out when the boys upset you. But how much actual, useful German do you understand?"

After shooting off my mouth to impress my wife, could I really read what my cousin had written? I turned to the opening page, sweating just a little. I guessed we'd find out.

CHAPTER 2

der 24. Juli 1936
Berlin, Germany

THREE MONTHS AGO, I WAS NAMED THE HEAVYWEIGHT CON-
*tender to represent Germany in boxing during the 1936
Summer Olympic Games. I cannot help but wonder how it
might feel to hear "Hans Pepperman" called out during the
medal ceremony. My good friend, Herbert Runge, is first alter-
nate. A week before the Olympics, the training regimen has
tapered off, but the constant ache in my knuckle has not...*

I hit the heavy punching bag with a hard-right cross.
A sharp sting bit me like a pit viper. Intuition rattled my
brain with negative thoughts. There was nothing good
about the pain in my hand. Nothing good.

An hour later, an x-ray confirmed my suspicion and
revealed a shattered knuckle.

Devastated couldn't begin to explain my disappointment. Back in my room at the training facility, I kicked
over a chair. "All the sparring." I ripped the covers off
my bed. "All the running." My muscles twitched. "All
the sweat." Heat flushed through my body. "All the long
hours." I slapped a newspaper off the desk with my good
hand. The pages fluttered and twisted to the floor. "For

nothing." I screamed and cursed until Runge ran into my room and grabbed me around the chest.

We had only been friends for a few months, but his presence calmed me as I sat on the bare mattress. "What will I tell Mama and Papa? And Papa's brother, Uncle Wilhelm, and his ten-year-old son Patrick who have come from the United States to watch me? I let them down." My eyes clouded. It was all I could do to hold back the tears.

Runge pulled up a chair across from me. He didn't try to give me answers. He listened, which was exactly what I needed. Exactly what a good friend would do.

CHAPTER 3

der 1. August 1936
Berlin, Germany

*L*IFE NEVER SEEMS FAIR, BUT THAT IS NOTHING NEW. *M*Y *O*LYMPIC *experience has been taken away, but I have been raised to face life's challenges head-on and not wallow in self-pity — so I am dressing in my uniform to march in the opening ceremony…*

People wearing their finest filled the seventy-thousand-seat arena. Both men and women wore white straw hats, the women's tilted to one side. Hand-painted wooden boxes overflowing with yellow, orange, and purple flowers lined the entrance. Flags of bright red, black, and white swayed in the summer breeze — the perfect weather for competition.

Overhead, whispering propellers gently pushed the Hindenburg across the blue sky and through a low-hanging cloud. Watching left me with an uneasy feeling. My chemistry professor had lectured about the dangers of using the flammable hydrogen instead of much safer helium. I closed my eyes, my breathing shallow and heavy. But I couldn't escape my erratic heartbeat or the image of that massive airship bursting into flames. Could it happen?

Struggling to rein in the horrible visual, I exhaled and focused on the German National anthem playing over the speakers. Forcing a smile, I nodded at Herbert Runge next to me.

"It's a great day to be a German." His chest swelled, and I felt his pride. "I'm honored to be representing my country, but it's bittersweet." He nodded toward my cast. "I'm sorry for your broken hand."

"I ask one thing, Herbert." I adjusted my hat, pulling it snug with my good hand. "Win the gold medal." What could have been, what should have been, my glory.

He placed his right fist over his heart and pounded. "I will not let you or my country down." Standing tall, he angled his chin upward in a show of determination.

If anyone had to replace me, I was glad the honor went to Runge. He had the will to win the gold. I hoped he had the skill. My loss was one thing but Germany's was another.

Across the arena, twenty-five thousand pigeons were being readied for release. When I'd read the article this morning in the *Berliner* newspaper, the number had astounded me. But as the cage doors opened and the birds shot skyward, my expectation was nothing compared to the actual event.

"Herbert, look." I pointed up.

With that many birds, I'd anticipated at least one mid-air collision. Not so. They scattered without a single mishap until the five-cannon salute.

The blast echoed off the concrete walls, bunching the flock together and — *splat, splat, splat* — scaring the poop out of them. Groans filled the stadium as people brushed blobs of white and black *scheisse* off their clothing.

Fortunately, my uniform and hat collected the junk. Some weren't so lucky. Their heads suffered the consequences.

So did Herbert. A glob of poop perched on his nose and another on his chin. He laughed and flicked the mess off his face.

"Be serious," I said. "Today is historic. This is the first time the Olympic flame has been relayed by runners all the way from Greece to the host city."

He looked over. "*Ja wohl*. I'm glad Germany is the first country for this special event. Over thirty-three hundred relayed the torch." Runge tilted his head from side to side. "You and I could have done it ourselves."

I gave him a good-natured slap on the back of his head. "Maybe with two or three more boxers."

Runge responded by thumbing his nose.

Today was a great day. Athletes from all over the world gathered to compete in friendly competition—a good thing. I looked forward to making new friends, especially from the American team.

Then I remembered the lecture from Max Haup, one of our boxing coaches and a Nazi-party fanatic.

He'd stood tall in front of us, as if he had been strapped to a 1x12 board. "You represent the German people, and you are to act accordingly. Do not associate with Jews or people of color. These people are inferior. *Der Fuhrer* makes this request."

Before I could say anything, we'd been dismissed.

I turned to Runge now, contemplating the coach's remarks. The men and women from other countries were part of the human race, just like us. "Why does Coach Haup believe one ethnic group is inferior to another?"

Herbert rubbed his hand over his mouth as if to get rid of a bad taste. "Some of the black athletes are phenomenal, I agree, but as far as associating with the Jews, that shouldn't happen."

I snapped my head in his direction. "Why would you say that?"

His drawn face and furrowed eyebrows caught me off guard. "You know the Jews withdrew all of their money from the German economy during World War I. Those traitors were the reason we lost."

The Jews had appeared to be against the German cause, and they had hurt the country economically, but…

"*Meine damen und herren, willkommnen,* to the Games of the XI Olympiad." The president of the Olympic committee interrupted our conversation.

But I couldn't stop thinking about what Herbert had said. *Had* the Jews sabotaged a German victory?

The opening ceremony ended in spectacular fashion with the crowd cheering and another round of cannon fire. A formation of BF 109 fighter planes flew over the stadium—the squadron low enough to drown out the cheers.

Pride swelled through my body. Proud to be a German was an understatement. As I marched out of the stadium with the athletes, the German military band played, heavy on the drums and trumpets. As we paraded by the band section, the powerful beat exploded, sending waves of excitement through me.

I headed toward the *Olympiastadion's* main entrance, near the clock tower, where I planned to meet my family. I'd never seen so many vendors in one place selling pretzels, beer, bratwurst, pickled cucumbers, and *scho-ka-kola*, a sport confectionery launched at the Olympics. The dark chocolate had a heavy dose of caffeine, and I liked it.

Mama and Papa would go home today, but Uncle Wilhelm and his son had come all the way from America and would stay to watch this year's games. My relatives from America had stayed with Mama and Papa after their ship had docked in Hamburg. Then they had all ridden the train to *Anhalter Bahnhof* in Berlin.

Spotting Uncle Wilhelm was easy. He looked the same as an old photograph I'd seen—a big man with huge legs, a thick neck, and broad shoulders. We were about the same height, but he had at least twenty pounds on me.

Arms open wide, he pulled me close, slapping my back with heavy hands. "*Guten tag*, Hans. This is my son, Patrick." His bass voice rang loud for all to hear.

"Sorry you can't box." The boy lowered his head and pawed the ground with his right foot, obviously disappointed for me. "You could have won the *goldmedaille*."

He mixed in some oddly pronounced German with his English, but I understood the message. The boy was no doubt a Pepperman, large-boned and big for his age. His short blond hair, blue eyes, and chiseled jawline were trademarks of the Pepperman *gruppe*.

"I like to fight too. Papa showed me how to jab twice with my left hand and throw a right cross." He took the last bite of his sausage. Mustard spread from one side of his face to the other, and the condiment glistened off

15

his two front teeth. "You want me to show you?" The fire in his tone said I'd better get ready.

"Sure." I got down on one knee and raised my left palm.

Patrick pulled tight fists next to his face, squinted, and took aim. *Pow. Pow. Pow.*

The young man's punch had a sting and left my palm covered in a mix of mustard and sausage grease.

My handkerchief came in handy.

Patrick looked up at me, big blue eyes almost popping out of his skull. "Hans, we came on this big, big, boat. It was the Man... Man..." He looked at his father.

Wilhelm said, "The Manhattan."

"Yes, the Manhattan, the biggest ship in the whole world," Patrick continued. "And do you know what else?"

"What?" I asked.

"The American Olympic team was on the same boat with us. And do you know who I saw?"

"Who?" I asked, loving every minute of the little guy's story.

"Jesse Owens... and... and... Glenn Cunningham... and Louis Zamparini."

I was afraid his eyes were going to pop out onto the concrete.

Patrick tugged on my trousers. "And something else, Hans."

I grinned. "What else, Patrick?"

"The runners ran around the ship every morning, and I got to run with them, but I couldn't beat 'em. Their legs were too long."

What kind of man would Patrick grow up to be? He reminded me of someone. I chuckled — it was me.

CHAPTER 4

der 19. August 1936
Berlin, Germany

AFTER THE OLYMPIC EVENTS EACH DAY, UNCLE WILHELM, Patrick, and I have visited and toured Berlin – the Brandenburg Gate, the Pergamon Museum, and the Berlin Zoological Garden. The museums were not a focal point for Patrick but with plenty of ice cream, he managed...

Walking next to me at the zoo, Patrick shadow boxed, then shoved his hands high into the air just as Runge had done when he'd won the gold medal. "Let's go back to the gorilla area. I want to see that big silverback again." He smiled, not just a happy smile, but one of admiration.

The smile I returned was no different. Young cousin Patrick and I had become friends. And I wished for more time with Wilhelm. His mannerisms reminded me of my dad's. His warm, friendly smile and soft-spoken words were characteristics of a kind giant. That being said, I wouldn't want to push the man beyond his limits.

The Olympics would be remembered differently by each person, but for me, I would never forget the time I spent with my family, Germany winning the most medals with eighty-nine, the torch ceremony, and the pigeon mess on Runge's face.

Two days after the Olympics ended, I took Uncle Wilhelm and Patrick to *Anhalter Bahnhof* where they boarded a train to Hamburg. From there, they would take a ship back to America.

Patrick lowered the window, leaned out, and waved. "I'll write you."

In the short time we'd been together, our bond had become strong. Sadness swirled in my heart as I wondered if I would ever see them again.

CHAPTER 5

der 12. Oktober 1936
Braunschweig, Germany

I HAVE BEEN TOO BUSY TO WRITE IN MY JOURNAL. FOR THE LAST two months, my masters' thesis in mechanical engineering has occupied all my time. The professors at Braunschweig Institute of Technology are pushing me to prove my theory on increasing the power output in existing aircraft engines, and I believe I am close...

Rat-a-tat-tat. Rat-a-tat-tat. A loud commotion outside broke my concentration.

I opened the window and set both of my hands on the frame.

Twenty or so students outside my first-story room gathered around a guy who looked like one of his drumsticks as he pounded on his snare. Some clapped with the rhythm or jumped up and down shaking their bodies while others shouted, "*Lob Deutschland, Lob Deutschland*" Praise Germany.

A few carried signs that read, "*Blut und Boden.*" Blood and Soil. Others held torches. The people and the creepy, sinister shadows reflecting off the building reminded me of a tribal ritual leading up to an animal sacrifice.

A beautiful girl flipped her long, honey hair, pointed her sign at me, and smiled. "*Herrenvolk… Herrenvolk.*" Master Race.

Her red skirt and white sweater pulled so tight I envisioned Aphrodite, the Greek goddess, and all I could think was — *Zowie* — an American expression I'd picked up at the Olympics.

Gold and orange leaves flew inside my window along with a cold wind that slapped me in the face. Still making eye contact with the shapely blonde, I cupped my hands and exhaled into my palms to warm my cheeks.

A crackling voice over a loudspeaker invited everyone to a political rally at Schadts Brewery and Gasthaus on Oelschaegern Street at 9 p.m. to support the National Socialist German Workers' Party. *Nazi.*

Ever since Adolph Hitler had become Chancellor in 1933, Germany had been promoting an extreme nationalistic attitude. There'd been nothing but talk of uniting the German people — even annexing all German-speaking areas such as the Sudetenland in Czechoslovakia.

The rumors of war made no sense. A great depression was finally over, and people were happy and enjoyed plenty of food.

Shaking my head, I closed the window, wrapped a tan scarf around my neck, and buttoned my brown wool sweater. The savory beef and *bier* plate Schadts served pulled me to leave my cluttered room more than the propaganda meeting, and I had just enough time to eat before the muster started.

I walked my bicycle down the hall and onto the sidewalk. The downtown area was a mile from my student dormitory. Streetlights and the bicycle path made the trip easy as I rode by students going to the gathering. I looked for the blonde whose beauty spiked my interest but had no luck and gave up, racking my bicycle outside Schadts.

Loud singing of *Deutschland, Deutschland über alles* came from across the street.

Two middle-aged *bier*-bellied imbeciles wearing Nazi armbands bumped into an elderly Jewish man as he locked up Rosheim's Clothing Store.

I held my breath, wondering if they were harmless drunks or if this would turn into something more.

One of the morons flipped the kippah off the Jew's head and kicked the hat into the busy street. Then they walked off, arms around each other's shoulders, laughing.

I let out a deep breath. I'd seen this pitiful, repulsive behavior before in Munich, but it hadn't ended so quickly. Who cared if the man was Jewish? Why couldn't people accept others for who they were?

The Jewish man recovered his cap. He pointed his fingers toward his own neck and forcefully flicked his fingers toward the men in disgust.

The old gentleman had spunk.

Good for him. Smiling, I pushed through the heavy oak door of Schadts to a crowd jammed around the huge, round wooden bar in deep discussions about how Germany was once again a strong, united country.

Nazi flags and posters of Hitler papered every wall. The rank odor of stale tobacco made me cough and almost spoiled my appetite.

I asked for a table near the back of the building.

A middle-aged woman dressed in a *dirndl* — a white apron and a dark blue skirt — with the forearms of a heavyweight boxer walked toward me. "Would you like a menu?" Her baritone voice matched her physique.

I shook my head. "*Nein.* I want the beef and *bier* and a mug of *Erdinger Kristall.*"

She turned her head to one side and gave me what I think she meant as a flirty smile. "Anything else?" Her eyebrows arched.

Sure she'd practiced that move many times in front of a mirror, I grinned. "*Nein.*" Her attempted seduction was nice, even if she wasn't my type.

The roast beef and potatoes in a dark *bier* sauce were better than Mama's, but I would never tell her that. Once my table was cleared, I slouched in my chair, ordered another *Erdinger,* and waited for the speaker.

A man who appeared to be in his thirties wearing a black suit and a Nazi armband climbed on top of the bar. "The Nazi Party has pledged to work for the common people. The party provides much needed jobs to get Germany's economy moving again. The unemployment rate is the lowest in thirty years." He pulled a handkerchief from his back pocket and dabbed at his stern, sweaty forehead.

He was right about the low unemployment rate. Many jobs were available, especially in the construction business.

The man loosened his tie. "Germany is taking its place among the great nations of the world. We are superior workers. No nation can out-produce the German people. *Der Fuhrer* has promised the *Das Dritte Reich* will last a thousand years. Join *Nationalsozialistische deutsche Arbeiterpartei*. Be part of the greatest nation the world has ever seen." He doubled one fist and pounded it into his open palm, over and over.

His "Third Reich, join the National Socialist German Workers' Party" speech lasted an hour and was peppered with grandiose hyperboles. By the time he finished, the fever-pitched crowd clanked glasses of *bier* and more of the golden liquid spilled on the floor than was consumed.

Could Hitler be our savior? Could I be mistaken about the Nazi Party? There was nothing wrong with taking pride in one's nation. Except... something in my gut wondered if Hitler's motives were more personal than political.

CHAPTER 6

der 4. Januar 1937
Stuttgart, Germany

I AM STILL STRUGGLING WITH THE PRINCIPLES OF THE NAZI Party. The nationalism I have no problem with, but how the party views other ethnic groups is an issue. It just does not feel right. Growing up, some of my best friends were Jews. Germany cannot go through another war. The people have no stomach for it. On to other news – the Daimler-Benz aircraft engine company has offered me a position. Boring out the cylinders to make the diameter larger did increase the power output from 1,332 to 1,455 horsepower in the Daimler-Benz 601 engine being used in the BF 109 fighter planes. I proved my theory…

I had been at the Daimler-Benz office in Stuttgart only a few days when my boss, Philip Baron, stopped by my door. His average build and thick gray hair reminded me of one of my university professors. Mr. Baron's PhDs in mathematics and mechanical engineering impressed me.

"Hans, I have an assignment for you. We got a call from the Bavarian Aircraft Works in Augsburg. Willy Messerschmitt, the chief designer of the BF 109 fighter, is having problems with the fuel injection. The plane flies well at altitudes under six thousand feet. But at six thousand feet and above, the engine sputters and cuts out during tight turns. He thinks this could be caused by a flaw in the system, not a maintenance issue. Bavarian Aircraft will send a plane for you."

I tapped my fingers on the desk. "Can I take a train instead?" Flying… in an airplane… not good. Not good at all.

He gave me a look, probably thinking not just *no* but *hell no.*

I never thought getting on a plane would be part of my job description, but I had only been here a few days and needed to be a team player. I took a deep breath and exhaled. "Yes, sir. When do I leave?"

"Seven in the morning." He slapped the door frame. "Be prepared to stay a while. Mr. Messerschmitt wants you to get a real feel for the BF 109. This is your chance to shine. Do not disappoint." Barron hesitated. He stepped into my office, shut the door, and sat in front of me. "Hans, no country has the technology to challenge the airframe of the BF 109, and the 601 engine has no equal. The fuel injection system is what makes the engine unique. Russia, in particular, has been trying to steal our secrets. Be watchful and suspicious of everyone." He shook my hand and left.

I didn't know how Barron knew about the spying, and I didn't ask. Another world war seemed imminent.

The alarm was set for 5:30 a.m., but I didn't need the reminder. I was already awake and had packed my suitcase the night before.

The Bosch Bakery around the corner from my apartment was handy for a cup of coffee, but I really stopped there for a slice of Black Forest cake. Three chocolate layers stuffed with cherry filling and topped with whipped cream, the delight was a bit rich for this early in the morning, but I didn't care.

A taxi met me at the bakery and drove me to the factory.

Januar meant fog and drizzle in Stuttgart. The sun tried to peek through the gray, low-hanging clouds, and the strange orangish glow added to my anxiety. Could this be an omen?

Shaking off the thought, I stepped out of the taxi, paid the driver, and entered the foyer carrying my suitcase. The reflection in the glass door showed off my new gray tweed suit and classy black tie. The pinch-crown gray wool fedora, cocked to one side, was stylish as well.

A small-framed, black-haired Luftwaffe officer approached me. "Are you Mither Pepperman?"

I tried not to react to his slight lisp. "Yes." I extended my right hand.

"Erich Hartmann, the pilot for your flight to Augthburg."

Was he old enough to be a German military pilot? He didn't even look old enough to be in the German Youth. "How long have you been flying?" I asked, even though I really didn't want to know.

"I graduated from pilot training last week. This is my second cross-country flight." He turned and headed to the exit door toward the landing strip, his steps as cocky as Joe Lewis, the American boxer.

Second cross-country flight? I froze. I was supposed to get on a plane and fly in the rain to Augsburg with a kid just out of flight school. "Hold up."

He did a sharp military about-face.

"You are the copilot, right?" I hoped my inquiry was accurate.

He angled his head with a puzzled look. "No, sir. Just me."

I supposed he could see the heavy dose of fear etched on my face as I felt the blood drain from my head so fast it made me dizzy.

"You don't have to worry, sir. I graduated first in my class and have been assigned to fighter pilot training. You're in capable hands." His confident, upturned smile and teenage voice gave me no security.

My feet scraped the concrete as we approached the two-seater scout plane parked next to the dull metal hanger. Shreds of mist hovered over the building, the entire scene ghostly.

Oh *scheisse*.

I lodged the suitcase behind the seat and twisted my body to get into the cramped cockpit.

Young Hartmann started the engine. The high-pitched *kling, kling, kling* was not a confidence builder. I'd heard more power generated by washing machines.

He taxied to the end of the runway, turned into the wind, and pushed the throttle forward. The timid roar of the engine increased and spurred into a howl of desperation.

Attempting to lift the plane into the air, the young airman barely had the wheels off the ground when the plane lurched downward, slamming on the airstrip, and bounced twice.

I bounced along with it, my head hitting the top of the cockpit, smashing my new fedora. *Scheise. Scheise. Scheise.*

He gave it more power and tried again to get airborne.

"Hail Mary, full of grace." I mumbled and crossed myself while Hartmann yawned as though the awkward takeoff was normal.

Looking down the runway, I noticed a grove of trees no more than four hundred yards away. We weren't going to make it over them.

Sweat beaded my forehead. I tapped my heels on the floor and gritted my teeth, looking at the pilot. Come on. Get this gooney bird into the air.

Hartmann's expression stayed calm as a mountain lake in summer.

I grabbed the sides of my seat and squeezed so hard my knuckles cracked, my life flashing in front of me.

The growling engine barely lifted us over the trees.

The air jockey stared straight ahead, but his grin told me he'd played the biggest practical joke on me that had ever been perpetrated.

Awkwardly, I slapped his arm with the back of my hand. "You did that on purpose."

His eyes narrowed, and his jawline locked tight as a medieval chastity belt. "Just wanted to get your day started off right."

"Well, your plan didn't work. I need to change my pants." Not really. But almost.

We both laughed.

My feeling about Erich Hartmann had changed. His military career was on the rise. His flight skills were medal worthy. And his humor — well, that was yet to be decided.

CHAPTER 7

der 4. Januar 1937
Augsburg, Germany

EXCEPT FOR THE INFREQUENT AIR POCKETS THAT JUMBLE MY
writing, the flight to Augsburg with young Hartmann could
not be easier. The fog burned off early, making the view spec-
tacular. The fast currents in the winding blue rivers take my
mind off flying. Maybe Hartmann laughing each time my
fedora slaps the top of the cockpit because of turbulence has
cured my fear of air travel...

A little after 9:00 a.m., we approached the Bavarian
Aircraft Works. I closed my journal to look at the row
of BF 109 fighter planes lining the tarmac. I couldn't
take my eyes off the magnificent airframes. The crisp,
sleek lines and long stout noses reminded me of a
great white shark. Both were predators. Both gave
me chills.

Hartmann asked me to wait in Willy Messerschmitt's
office. The chief designer of the BF 109 had a desk cluttered with aircraft designs and blueprints. The walls
were covered with pictures of Hitler and other digni-
taries shaking hands with Messerschmitt.

The stench of his stuffed ashtray irritated my nose. I took a seat and angled my chair away from the mound of half-smoked cigarettes.

The longer I sat waiting, the more I questioned my ability to do this job. All sorts of arrows and darts poked at my confidence. What if I couldn't solve the fuel injection problem? What if I made it worse? What if Daimler fired me because of ineptitude? My throbbing pulse drummed in time with my laboring heart.

Several airplanes revved outside Messerschmitt's office. The high-pitched whine conjured an image of fierce attack planes.

"Get that *verdammt* engineer from Daimler down here immediately." The deep voice from down the hall captured my attention. "The fuel injection problem has got to be solved."

Several deep breaths almost helped ease my anxiety — until the door burst open.

A man of average height stormed around the desk and plopped down across from me in a cushioned black leather chair. He grabbed a cigarette from his shirt pocket, jammed it into his mouth, and flicked a lighter several times before lighting the tobacco stick. "And who might you be?" Inhaling and exhaling a stream of smoke straight up, he watched me with eyes that could ignite a lump of coal.

I was not going to be intimidated. Leaning forward, I met his dark, emotionless gaze head-on. "I'm the man who is going to resolve the fuel injection problem in the 109." I hoped.

Messerschmitt flipped the top of the silver lighter. *Click. Click. Click.* His stare seemed to go on forever.

I had a feeling most people kowtowed to this man, but I wasn't going to be one of them. I kept my focus and refused to blink.

"What's your name?" He lifted the cigarette to his lips and took another drag. This time he blew the smoke from the corner of his mouth, all the while flipping the lighter top. *Click. Click. Click.*

My stare still narrowed in on his. I tightened my jaw the way I did right before I stepped into the ring. "Hans Joachim Pepperman." I gave him a hard look to let him know his bullying tactics wouldn't work on me.

He leaned back in his chair, dropping both arms next to his sides, still holding onto his lighter. *Click. Click. Click.* "Hans Pepperman, the Olympic boxer?" A bland mask of indifference crossed his face.

I slowly nodded. "The same."

He picked a piece of tobacco off the tip of his tongue. "Go check into the hotel. You start tomorrow at 8:00 a.m." He grabbed a blueprint and swiveled his chair away from me in quick dismissal.

What an arrogant *trottel*.

CHAPTER 8

der 4. Januar 1937
Augsburg, Germany

The initial meeting with Messerschmitt enlightened me. His self-assured, pompous disposition is loathsome. However, his no-nonsense attitude matches mine. Maybe we are too much alike. He does not think I can correct the problem with the fuel injection system. That is all the motivation I need…

The cool, crisp winter day was a bit of a reprieve from the freezing, nasty days associated with this part of Bavaria. Even the skeleton-like fingers of the tree branches outside my hotel window seemed to push upward toward the clear, blue sky, relishing the break from the bitter weather.

Hartmann had driven me to the Hotel Baur, my home until Daimler-Benz recalled me to Stuttgart. The old, stately stone structure impressed me. The elegance of the Baur oozed with power and wealth — its eccentric, over-the-top luxury pretentious.

I slid my journal into a drawer by the bed and unpacked the fuel injection system schematics from the bottom of my suitcase. My room was small and plain, but I had a table where I could work. I didn't want to waste time.

The sooner I solved the problem and proved my worth to Messerschmitt as a mechanical engineer, the better.

As I laid the blueprints out, the same doubt I'd felt before winning my first boxing championship latched onto me. This was my first job, and it was important to succeed. The thought of failure hung heavier than a mill-stone tied around my neck. I must get to work.

Time escaped me. My stomach growled. I checked my watch, surprised to find lunch was over, and I was about to miss dinner. So far, I'd found nothing that would indicate why the fuel injection system would cut out. Hopefully, a full stomach would refresh me.

Pushing back from the desk, I stretched and put on the tweed coat and cinched my tie. I rubbed the knuckle I broke before the Olympics to ease the ache.

As I approached a man and woman next to the elevator, the man greeted me. "*Guten abend.*"

"*Guten abend,*" I returned the evening greeting politely.

The lady entered the elevator first, followed by her escort, and her gaze caught mine. Dark eyes and ruby lips captivated me. Her sculptured cheek bones and short, brown hair were stunning. But it was the way she undressed me with her eyes that caught me off guard and captured my full attention.

I went to the back of the elevator and positioned myself for a better take.

The view did not disappoint. Her body curved in all the right places, her small waist and shapely calves sculptured to perfection.

Trapped in the woman's beauty, I followed her and the man off the elevator.

As she reached the front door of the hotel, she turned her head. The slow smile she gave me had the power to stop a runaway train sprinting down a steep slope.

To say I was interested would be an understatement.

"Hans… Hans Pepperman."

I turned toward the voice calling my name.

"How about a *bier*?" Eric Hartmann stood in front of the entrance to the bar.

"Sure." I had already taken a liking to the guy, and a *bier* with the only person I knew in Augsburg was welcomed. "You owe me a drink after that takeoff from Stuttgart."

My remark triggered a laugh that made Hartmann sound like an ornery teenager.

The large bar was filled with heavy wood tables and thickly padded high-back chairs, not at all like the food-stained bare tables and broken-down chairs I was used to. I didn't feel uncomfortable, but the motif was not to my liking. Neither were the guests as they walked around me, their haughty noses peaked upward as though they were better than everyone else. If Daimler had not been covering my expenses, I could not afford one night here.

The tables were filled, so Hartmann and I took the last two seats at the bar.

"*Was mochten sie trinken?*" The bartender, dressed in a starched white shirt and black bow tie had slicked-back oily brown hair and a pencil-thin mustache. His deep baritone voice had a mellow, hypnotic sound reminding me of Lucifer in Dante's *Inferno*.

"Two WeihenstephanWeiss *biers*." Hartmann apparently hadn't noticed the bartender's strangeness. "Is that okay with you?"

I forced a smile. "You're buying."

He gave me a smug grin and nodded to the bartender who lifted his head and looked at me in a way I wasn't sure I wanted to interpret.

When the bartender turned away, Hartmann leaned a little closer and lowered his voice. "Be careful what you say and do here. The Gestapo headquarters is located on the second floor. Those people would all take a dagger for Hitler and the Third Reich. The bar area is always filled with Gestapo personnel. I've heard the bar lavatory is wired. I do not know if that is true or not."

As if the bartender heard, he turned toward me, his gaze piercing with sinister calculation. Although his tongue was not forked, the tip slipped between his lips as though testing the air.

Could he be a Gestapo agent?

Hartmann knocked the bar in front of me to get my attention. "I just found out from some of the other pilots you were a boxer."

I flexed the fingers on my right hand. "I am a boxer."

The look on Hartmann's face was priceless. "Are you going to hit me for scaring you this morning?"

The bartender placed two *biers* on napkins. The bubbly, white foam spilled over and ran down the sides of the sparkling, clean glasses.

"No." I took a sip. The clean taste was refreshing and just what I needed. "But, if I fly with you again and you do that crazy touch-and-go takeoff, I will." I doubled my fist and shook it at him.

He placed both hands in front of his face. "Not to worry. Not to worry."

I waved to the bartender, hesitant to even bother the man again. "Can I order a sandwich?"

"Do you need a menu, sir?" The arrogant way he slurred *sir* was as phony as his mustache.

"No, I want a Rueben on pumpernickel."

He wiped his hands on a white towel, walked to a waiter, and placed my order.

I looked at Hartmann. "How about you?"

"I'm going to enjoy a liquid meal tonight." He finished his *bier* in two gulps and a loud burp. Grinning, he scratched the top of his head, reminding me of Stan Laurel in the Laurel and Hardy movies.

We sat at the bar for several hours. Most of the conversation centered on the BF 109.

"When does the engine seem to cut out?" I asked.

Hartmann sipped a fresh wheat *bier* and pondered the question. "At six thousand feet and in a tight turn."

"Does the engine stall?"

"No, it just loses power."

I tugged my lower lip, thinking about his response. "We'll talk some more. Right now, I have a bladder problem, and I do have an answer for that." I stepped back from the stool and — *wham* — crashed into someone.

A lady made a shrill sound and fell into a waiter carrying a tray of drinks. Glass shattered across the room.

I turned.

The beautiful lady from the elevator was sprawled on the floor, her porcelain face frozen in shock, her dress up to her waist.

CHAPTER 9

der 4. Januar 1937
Augsburg, Germany

I FEEL TERRIBLE ABOUT WHAT HAPPENED AT THE BAR TONIGHT.
People rushed to help the lady I accidentally knocked down.
When I tried to apologize, the man who had been with her on
the elevator pushed me away. In all the commotion, I did not
even get her name. Hopefully, I will have another chance…

I took a shower, set the alarm clock, and slid under soft, white linen sheets.

At 3:45, I shot up in bed, my heart double-timing. What if the fuel injector was not the problem? My chuckle started low and soft, then crescendoed loud and hard. One of my favorite physics professors, Lars "Dr. Mouse" Wartes, always said, "Never assume a problem to be a major one. Start with a simple solution and work forward."

I flung the covers back, found my pants, and pulled the pockets inside out. What happened to the piece of paper Hartmann gave me with his *telefon* number? I checked my wallet. Not there. My shirt. Where was my shirt?

It lay in a crumpled mass next to the desk.

I picked up the shirt and found the paper with the number. Dressing in the same clothes I'd worn yesterday, I ran to the elevator and slapped the down button. "Come on. Come on."

The cables clanged, and the passenger box jolted. An eternity passed before the doors opened.

Inside the elevator, I pushed the lobby button three times, as though that would get the elevator to move faster. Jamming both hands into my pants pockets, I checked for change. None there. I felt around in my jacket pocket and pulled coins out, enough to make a call.

The elevator doors sprung open. I stepped out looking right, then left for the *telefon* booth. Ah, next to the bar entrance.

I ran across the lobby, opened the *telefon* booth door, and slammed it shut. Picking up the receiver, I dropped the coins into the slot and dialed the number.

One ring. Two. And three.

"Hartmann, answer the phone."

He picked up on ring number four. "Erich Hartmann, *guten tag*."

The way he slurred his words, I hoped it was his lisp, and he wasn't drunk. "Erich, this is Hans."

"Who?"

"Hans Pepperman. Meet me at the hotel." After a short pause, I heard the squeaking coils of his box springs.

"It's four in the morning."

"I know what time it is. I need you to drive me to the Bavarian Aircraft Works."

"What? Why do you want…?"

"Get over here right now, or I'll beat you senseless."

"I'll be right over." The slur disappeared.

I paced back and forth outside the Baur, the morning air cold and filled with tiny bits of sparkling ice crystals. What if I fixed the engine my first day on the job? I doubled both fists and shadow boxed — two left jabs and a knockout right cross.

A lone car approached the hotel. Had to be Hartmann. The car stopped.

I jerked open the door and plopped onto the front seat.

His shirt had so many creases it looked like he'd wadded it up before putting it on. His hair spiked in every direction. His breath smelled like the bottom of a tuna fish can.

"Rough night?" I reached over and slapped his shoulder.

He flinched, and the car almost went off the road.

"Never mind." I shook my head. "Just get me to the Bavarian Air Works. This could be a great day."

"Whatever you say." He yawned, exposing me again to another blast of year-old tuna that could melt rocks.

We pulled up to the gate entrance of the aircraft works and showed our passes to the military guard.

He waved us through.

"Go to the hangar with the 109s," I told Hartmann, "and take me to the plane you fly."

The car slowed, and he looked at me. "What are you going to do to my plane?"

"I'm going to put a time bomb under the seat and blow it up. What do you think I'm going to do, *Dummkopf*?

I'm going to solve the cutting-out problem at six thousand feet."

Hartmann scratched his cheek. "My momma's going to be mad at you if you blow up my plane."

The young fighter pilot had a dry sense of humor. I would be his wing commander any day.

"What time do the mechanics arrive? I'll need their help to locate some tools."

"My guess would be around 8:00 a.m."

"That will give me time to look over the engine schematics one more time."

Hartmann left me to it.

One of the mechanics arrived early and helped me locate the tools to work on the D. B. 601 engine.

At 7:30, I closed the cowling on the plane, washed my hands, and headed to Messerschmitt's office. I wanted to be outside his door when he arrived.

As he turned the corner and noticed me seated outside his office, he hesitated, maybe surprised to see me. He took the keys from his pocket and unlocked the door, tilting his head to motion me inside. "I'll show you to your office as soon as I get some coffee."

Pompous *arsch*. "I don't need to go to my office." My next remark would be premature, but I couldn't resist. "I've solved the problem with the fuel injection system."

He slowly set his briefcase on the floor and turned. "What did you say?" It wasn't that he hadn't heard me. He just didn't believe me.

"I said... I've solved the problem with the fuel injection system." Truth be known, I didn't know for sure. I would either be a hero or a goat. If my hypothesis didn't work, I would be back in Stuttgart before dark. But if my hypothesis was right, that self-assertive SOB would be humbled, my gamble well worth the risk.

He sat at his desk, pulled out a cigarette, and lit the tobacco.

Hard to decide what was worse — the stink of Messerschmitt's cigarette or Hartmann's tuna breath.

"Let me see the schematics." He tapped his index finger on the desk. Hard. "Point out the problem, and how you fixed it."

I set the blueprints in front of him but instead of pointing down, I turned and pointed to the door. "I've already worked on Hartmann's plane. He's ready to take it up now."

Messerschmitt placed his hands on the desk and pushed out of the chair, cigarette dangling from the corner of his frowning mouth. "So, you're not going to tell me the problem." He took a deep drag and angrily exhaled a mist of spit. "I like your confidence." He smashed the cigarette into the empty tray. "You'd better be right."

Knees weak, I swallowed hard as we walked toward the hangar. I'd banked everything on a hunch. That was so unlike me. But I'd be damned if I let Messerschmitt know just how much he intimidated me.

Leaning against his plane, Hartmann crossed his arms and legs, the cocky pose typical. He looked much better than he had an hour ago with his hair combed and his flight suit unwrinkled and clean.

"Take her up to six thousand feet," Messerschmitt said. "Do tight turns. Don't hold back."

"*Jawohl.*" His "yes, sir" rang out crisp and strong.

A crowd of people filed out from the hangar and office building — men dressed in coats and ties, women in skirts and sweaters, other men in jumpsuits.

How had the word gotten out?

Every eye appeared to bore down on me. Like I needed more pressure. *Scheisse!*

Hartman climbed into the cockpit, pulled on his aviator cap, fastened his seat belt harness, and turned over the powerful 601 engine.

The prop wash kicked bits of dirt and a few dried leaves off the concrete.

He taxied down the runway and turned into the wind, revving the engine to takeoff speed. The predator plane lumbered slowly at first, but quickly picked up the pace, faster and faster, until the plane was airborne.

The airship remained visible for only a few minutes before it disappeared.

The crowd grew quiet. Ghostly quiet. The only sound was the caw of ravens in the distance.

Could the bird chatter be a bad omen? *Thump. Thump. Thump.* I heard my pounding heart. I looked at Messerschmitt.

His motionless body went rigid, and he pushed his hands deep into his black overcoat. His wind-swept hair exposed a receding hairline, and the breeze popped the German flag on the pole next to the office building.

The silence was numbing. Were the workers expecting failure? Would I be ridiculed if my assumptions were wrong?

I looked at my watch. 8:45. How long would it take Hartmann to reach six thousand feet and make his high-speed turns?

I looked at my watch again. 9:00.

The onlookers mumbled.

Where was Hartmann? He'd been gone too long. Had he crashed?

A nervous twitch spasmed my left eye.

A screaming whistle blasted from the 109 that flew not more than two hundred feet above our heads. Hartmann rocked the wings back and forth, telling me no mechanical problems.

The crowd erupted with shouts of joy.

A rush of adrenaline spread through my anxious body. I looked at Messerschmitt.

His body language changed in a heartbeat. His slight grin turned to a full-blown gleam of white teeth, and he slapped my back twice. "Well done, young man. Well done. Let's go back to my office. Tell me what you discovered." He walked back toward the hangar as though a boxcar of iron had been lifted off his tired body.

I took a deep breath and eased air out of my nose. I couldn't wait for Hartmann to tell us how the plane performed. This was a good day. No. A *herrlich* day. On the way to Messerschmitt's office, I stopped by the washroom and splashed cold water on my face. My reflection in the mirror over the sink exposed my condition. Red eyes, drawn cheeks, and black stubble gave me away as exhausted and emotionally spent.

Many more sorties would have to be flown to prove my hypothesis, but the first test had been a positive one indeed.

Knocking on Messerschmitt's door and walking in was much easier this time.

He hung up the phone.

"Come in, Pepperman. Take a chair. Do you want something to drink?"

"No, sir. I'm fine." This couldn't be the same man who had greeted me yesterday.

"Get to the point. Tell me about the problem with the fuel injector and spare me the engineering details."

I adjusted my chair to be directly in front of his. "The problem's not the fuel injector."

He leaned forward, overlapping his hands. "It's not the fuel injector?"

"No. The problem is related to the oil pump not having enough oil. At high altitudes, the oil foams. I topped off the coolant system with a quarter liter of oil. But that's only a stopgap measure to prove my point."

"So, what's the final solution?"

"It could be replacing the roller bearings in the pump. We also have to increase the oil pressure and use a better grade of oil. I have some ideas. If those don't work, a new oil pump will have to be designed. I'll go back to Stuttgart. If Daimler will allow me, I'll start to work immediately."

"No, you won't." Messerschmitt shook his head, resting his elbows on the desk and steepling his fingers.

"Sir?"

"I just got off the phone with Baron. You're staying in Augsburg. I want you here. If your hypothesis is right about the oil and the roll bearings in the fuel injectors, Russia and other adversaries will give anything for this information. It must be kept secret. Let's go forward and prove your theory. I have seven other 109s. What would you say if we topped off the oil pumps on three more planes, left the other four with no added oil, and see what happens?"

"That's a good idea." I nodded. But was it a good idea? What if Hartmann's plane had been a fluke? What if all the planes sputtered out?

The exciting adrenaline rush turned into a metallic taste in the back of my mouth, choking me.

CHAPTER 10

der 6. Januar 1937
Augsburg, Germany

YESTERDAY'S TEST FLIGHT ENCOURAGED ME. I FEEL LIKE I AM
on the right track with the 109. Regardless of the success or
failure of the test flights today, I want to look into using a
better grade of oil and replacing the roller bearings in the oil
pump. Did not sleep much last night…

I paced in front of the hotel elevator, anxious to get
to the Airworks factory for the morning trials.

The carrier stopped on the third floor, the doors
opened, and there in front of me stood the beautiful lady
I'd knocked over two nights ago.

Our eyes locked, and she smiled. And not just an
ordinary smile. No, a smile that turned me into jelly-
fish glob. She angled her head ever so slightly. "Are
you going to knock me down again?" Her silky voice
matched her beautiful dark eyes.

I couldn't stop staring. Her mellow voice mesmerized me. "Yes, ma'am."

Her chin dipped. "You're going to run over me again?"

Realizing my stupid mistake, I shook my head.
"*Nein… Nein.* I'm so sorry about the other night."

"Well, that's a relief." She smiled again.

The elevator door started to close.

I slapped my hand against the metal frame.

She stepped out and walked down the hall.

"Wait. Wait a minute." I walked after her. "What's your name?"

She stopped and pivoted toward me. "Anna Beck." She extended a right hand with neatly filed red nails.

"Hans Pepperman." I cupped her soft, warm palm in mine, surprised at the almost-electrical surge that raced through my body.

"Nice to meet you, *Herr* Pepperman." Her words were dry. She obviously wasn't feeling the same surge, but I couldn't stop looking at her. To say her beauty didn't captivate me would be disingenuous, but it wasn't just her beauty. It was her total presence. Her confident manner. And a face that made me want to lose myself in her.

"*Herr* Pepperman." She glanced toward our interlocking hands.

I'd made a fool of myself again. Nothing to lose now. I let go of her hand and cleared my throat. "Would you like to have a drink after work?"

Her long stare held no emotion, then her mouth parted in a slight grin. "I would like that."

"Five-thirty in the hotel bar?"

Without saying a word, she nodded, turned, and walked down the hall, her perfectly shaped legs carrying her effortlessly, almost catlike, to her room. As she unlocked the door, she gave me one last look. A look with no feeling.

Verdammt! My chest tightened. What she did to me.

My day at the Bavarian Aircraft plant turned out *wunderbar*. The three 109s with topped-off oil performed magnificently at six thousand feet. There'd been no problems with high-speed turns, and the engines hadn't cut out. It felt almost as good as being named to the German National boxing team. And the pivotal point of the day — Messerschmitt's attitude toward me changed.

I wanted to be of value to the genius aircraft designer. If Daimler would allow me to stay in Augsburg, that would be fine. The job was important. But now I had another reason to stay. Anna Beck most definitely piqued my interest.

I boarded the train next to the aircraft factory that would take me within three blocks of the Bauer Hotel.

The shrill sound of hissing steam followed by a high-pitched whistle warned everyone the train was departing.

When I stepped off at the Rathausplatz Station, the sharp sting of a winter blast assaulted my face and penetrated the collar of my shirt. I grasped the nape of my overcoat, pulling it tight against my neck.

The polished-brick pavement was slick from the bitter cold, but cautious steps pulled me faster and faster toward the Bauer Hotel, Anna's face going through my mind.

A sudden chill rolled down my back that had nothing to do with the wind. I stopped dead in my tracks as though a wall had been dropped in front of me. Twice I'd seen Anna on the third floor — my floor — of the hotel. Was she a guest? Or was she there for other reasons? Gestapo reasons?

As I rounded the corner toward the Bauer, my pace slowed.

A sizable crowd gathered in front of the hotel. Porters dressed in red jackets with black stripes around the cuffs, round furry hats, black pants, and spit-shined black shoes opened the doors for people stepping out of cars with their luggage.

I unbuttoned my overcoat in the lobby and made a quick swipe over my ruffled hair as I looked for Anna at the tables up front in the bar.

She wasn't there.

I was disappointed. Had she forgotten?

A small group of people moved, and I spotted her at the rear of the lounge with her back to the wall.

She lifted her hand and beckoned me.

As I walked closer, she stood, adjusting her tight skirt over her hips.

Wow.

She eased back into her chair. "I've ordered two *Weiss biers*. Hope that's suitable for you."

Anna was presumptuous in ordering for me. I liked that about her. "Of course." Wondering how to open the conversation, feeling like I'd never been on a date, I removed my overcoat and sat across from her.

"So, what brings you to Augsburg?" She took the initiative.

"I work for Daimler-Benz in Stuttgart. The company sent me here to work on a project at Bavarian Aircraft."

"Are you a pilot? You look too big to fit into those little airplanes."

"*Nein.* A mechanical engineer."

Anna straightened in her chair. "I'm impressed. Can you tell me about the project?"

"It's classified."

"I understand. So what university did you attend?"

"Braunschweig Institute of Technology. My life's pretty boring. Not many people want to know about technical things. What brought you to Augsburg?" I had to ask. She'd given me a perfect segue.

"I work for the government. If you think your life is boring…"

The wall dropped back in front of me. "What branch?"

"Gestapo."

And there it was. I sat back in my chair, folding both arms across my chest. I shifted, unable to get comfortable. "Are you an agent?"

Anna tilted her head back and laughed. "*Nein*. Clerical work."

"So, the Gestapo headquarters is in this hotel?" I knew the answer. I just wanted confirmation.

"Yes, the second floor, but my office is on the third. We ran out of space."

"That explains why I keep running into you at the elevator. No pun intended."

Anna nodded and smiled.

The waiter brought us the *biers*, and we toasted. The longer we sat and talked, the more I liked this woman. There was nothing pretentious about her, and I felt at ease in her presence.

She took a sip of *bier*, then slowly set her glass to the table, her warm, cheerful demeanor turning ice cold.

"What's wrong?" Had I done something? Said something?

"There's a man coming," she said under her breath. "A Gestapo agent out of my office. I can't make him understand there's nothing between us."

I gripped my drink.

The man bumped into my shoulder, and *bier* sloshed over my glass. "Oh, I'm so sorry, sir. Let me buy you another." He took the empty chair next to Anna and snapped his fingers. "*Barmann,* two more *biers.*" His ape-like eyebrows and crooked, pitted nose reminded me of a man in a circus sideshow. "And what might your name be?" He leaned over the table.

His arrogant tone and posture spiked my blood pressure. He was trying to intimidate me, and that didn't sit well. Neither did Anna's reaction to him.

Her spine was stiff as rebar. She looked straight ahead, not moving a muscle.

"Hans Pepperman." I answered the question, my voice cold.

He sniffed and scrunched his flat, scarred nose. "Heinrich Adler." He extended a meaty right hand with fingernails chewed to the quick.

I took a sip of *bier.* "Your first name again? I wasn't paying attention."

He sniffed once more and looked at me with dead-fish eyes. "*Hein-rich.*" He emphasized each syllable, setting a hand on Anna's and stroking it.

She made a fist and jerked her hand away.

"Ah, Heinrich. Such a forgettable name." My tone went from chilly to heated. "Here's what you're going to do. Get your *arsch* out of that chair and leave. Do you understand?"

He leaned back, stunned. His pause lingered. His breathing peaked. His nostrils flared.

I lifted my thumb and motioned toward the door.

He moved his chair away from the table, stood, adjusting his coat. "I'll be seeing you around. You can count on it."

Anna tapped an index finger on her glass and took a sip. "I've never heard anyone talk to Heinrich the way you did. Most people are afraid of him. That man has a psychotic nature."

I took my last sip and set the glass down. "I've been around people like him before. And his type doesn't concern me."

The *barmann* approached our table with two more *biers*. I needed to break the tension. "I should have let that brute Heinrich pay for our drinks before running him off."

Anna grinned, exposing shiny, white teeth. "Poor timing on your part."

"Where's your hometown, Anna."

"Garmisch."

"I bet you love to ski."

"Of course, don't you?"

"*Nein*. I'm from Hamburg. Not many mountains close by. If my father took us on a vacation, we'd go to a beach on the Baltic Sea. He liked to fish, and I enjoyed swimming in the cold waters."

"What does your father do for a living?" Anna tilted her glass.

"He's an auto mechanic. Worked on engines with him ever since I can remember."

"You inherited your technical thinking from your father."

I nodded. "I suppose."

We talked for two hours, but it seemed only minutes. "Anna, would you like to have dinner some evening?"

"I'd love to." She opened her purse, pulled out a note-pad, and wrote her address and phone number. When she handed it to me, she held onto the slip of paper for a moment before letting go.

What did that mean?

"I'm available most Friday nights. Please call."

She didn't have to remind me. I watched her every step as she left the room.

Leaving the lounge, I spotted the Gestapo goon at the end of the bar.

Heinrich's laughter stopped when he noticed me. He raised a stein in a challenge I'd eventually be forced to deal with.

A gut feeling told me he was trouble. I wasn't looking for a fight. But I wasn't running from one either.

CHAPTER 11

der 12. Januar 1937
Augsburg, Germany

I HAVE BEEN TOO BUSY TO WRITE THE LAST FEW DAYS. I TESTED the new oil for the oil pump, and it works fine, but I still feel the pump needs to be replaced to increase the oil pressure. Hopefully, the journal bearings, the simplest bearing with no roller element, will solve the pressure problem in the fuel injection...

In one corner of the breakroom, a group sang an off-key *Happy Birthday* to a coworker. Afterward, the mumbled chatter returned to normal.

"Excuse me, are you Hans Pepperman?" A gentleman who appeared to be in his early thirties, with thinning red hair and thick glasses, stood over my lunch table with a chipped, gray metal lunch box, his shoulders slightly slumped.

I closed the magazine I was reading. "I am." I pushed the publication aside.

"My name is Ernst Fischer. Sorry to disturb you."

We shook hands

"Please have a seat, Mr. Fischer." I gestured to the seat across from me. "You're not disturbing me at all. In fact, I'd enjoy your company."

He sat and pulled out a sandwich. When he unwrapped the wax paper, the odor reminded me of Uncle Rupert's outhouse — Limburger cheese with a golden sweet gherkin. The gherkin smelled almost as bad as the cheese. "Would you like half, Hans?" He rubbed his palms together as though he couldn't wait to eat.

"*Nein*. I just finished a bowl of potato soup."

He took a bite, and the cheese spread fell on the table. *Splat. Splat. Splat.* He followed up with a crunch of the sweet gherkin. Juice ran down his chin. A quick swipe with the back of his hand saved the liquid from joining the repulsive cheese on the table.

I tried not to look.

The employees seated at the next table packed their lunches and left.

"*Herr* Pepperman, you're becoming quite well-known. Everyone's talking about your marvelous work with the 109 engine."

"Thank you for the compliment." Truth be known, I'd gotten lucky. "What's your line of work?"

"Aircraft design engineer. I've worked extensively with the first 109 prototype."

I nodded. "That's one beautiful airplane."

He adjusted his glasses as if my comment embarrassed him and took another bite of his disgusting sandwich. Before he could swallow, he choked, coughed, and spewed the mixture all the way to my side of the table.

I leaned back in my chair. The guy was gross but seemed nice, so I forced a smile.

"I'm sorry, Hans." He reached across and raked bits of food to his side. "Please forgive my table etiquette." He coughed again, but this time his empty hand prevented the food from erupting like an active volcano. He cleared his throat, wiped his mouth with a semi-white handkerchief. "Are you going to the Nazi Party Rally today?"

A propaganda speech was the last thing I wanted to hear. "I suppose I will, but I'm not into politics."

Ernst looked right, left, and leaned forward. "Me neither," he whispered. "I think the people in control of our government are *nusse.* The only reason I'm going is because Messerschmitt's a strong follower of the *Fuhrer.* I joined the party to keep my job." He looked around again and straightened in his chair. "Are you a member?"

"*Nein.* And I don't ever intend to be."

Ernst slapped the table with a soft hand. "Good for you. You can be a true German citizen and love our country without following the racist philosophy of powerful government officials." He tapped the crystal on his watch. "It's time to get back to work." He gobbled down another bite of sandwich, stuffed the rest into his lunch pail, and pushed back from the table.

"One other thing before you go, Ernst. Are you familiar with the *Fuggerei* housing project in Augsburg?"

His eyebrows arched as he angled his head. He seemed surprised. "Of course, that's where I live. Why are you asking?"

"No reason," I lied. "I've heard it has nice living quarters." *Fuggerei* was the name Anna had written on her notepad.

Shrugging, Ernst stuck out his hand. Realizing gunk still covered his fingers, he pulled it back, wiped his hands on his olive pants, and walked out of the lunchroom.

I went back to my office but couldn't concentrate. Anna dominated my thoughts.

At 3:00 p.m., people shuffled outside in the hall. Rally time.

I went to the door and opened it. Leaning against the frame, I took a deep breath, and exhaled a huge puff of warm air. Just what I wanted to do—listen to some egotistical, brainwashed puppet programmed to extol the virtues of a political party of hate. I put on my coat, shut the door, and followed the other sheep down the hall.

The room was half full, but people were still coming in.

I looked to the front where a microphone was set up. And who do you suppose was sitting in a chair next to Willy Messerschmitt?

None other than Heinrich Adler.

It was as though there was no one in the room but the two of us. We locked onto each other like two male grizzlies ready to fight. He rolled his jaw and faked a spit on the floor. A definite challenge.

Our relationship was going to get interesting. And not in a positive way.

Adler's gibberish lasted about thirty minutes—the same boring gibberish I'd heard many times from like-minded propagandists, the speech filled with words about the superiority of the German people.

The meeting ended with *Deutschland Uber Alles*. As the voices grew louder singing the German National anthem, I slipped out and headed back to my office to get my briefcase. The only good that had come from the gathering was that the workday ended early.

As I waited to board the train back to the Bauer Hotel, snow fell. People bunched together like cattle from the frigid air blasts.

Someone nudged me from behind, then stepped next to me. "*Herr* Pepperman, I didn't know you worked for Bavarian Aircraft." Heinrich Adler jammed his black fedora almost to his bushy eyebrows and planted his hands deep into his overcoat pockets. "You provide a valuable service for the Fatherland."

"I'm employed by Daimler-Benz. I'm here for a project."

"Ah, and what project would that be, *Herr* Pepperman?"

I gave him a hard stare.

He rocked his head from side to side. "I understand. Hush, hush work." He paused. "We got off on the wrong footing. I misjudged you. Could we start over?" He extended his right hand.

I didn't trust this Gestapo thug, so I wasn't sure why I shook his hand.

"*Gut, gut.*" The train pulled to a stop. "Maybe we can sit and have a *bier* soon." He boarded.

The crowd pushing in after him gave me an excuse not to answer. When he'd seen me at the meeting today, his distaste had been obvious.

What changed? Why was he friendly now? It didn't sit right with me at all.

CHAPTER 12

der 15. Januar 1937
Augsburg, Germany

I AM IN A QUANDARY. IMPROVING THE ENGINE IN THE 109 WILL give Germany a superior fighter plane… but it will also benefit the Nazi Party. How can I remain loyal to my country without helping perpetuate a political party I despise? Philip Baron, my boss at Daimler-Benz, asked me to come to his office tomorrow. I am taking the train to Stuttgart tonight, and I will get my car and some personal belongings before I head in to see him. I need time to think…

Maybe Baron wanted to congratulate me on solving the fuel injection problem, and I hoped he wanted to give me a raise for my efforts. I arrived at his office at 9:00 a.m. Thirty-five minutes later, I was still listening to the roar of engines and counting airplanes passing over the building.

Finally, Baron opened his door and motioned me inside. The room hadn't changed in the last two weeks. The same empty champagne bottle with a wilted boutonniere stuck in the top highlighted the credenza behind his desk.

A stranger stood near the window in the corner of the room smoking a pipe, the tobacco aroma an unusual cherry fragrance. His short, bulky frame, thick Hitler mustache, and combed-back oily black hair screamed middle-management. The buttons of his suit jacket pulled so tight against his bulging stomach that the fabric threatened to tear.

"Have a seat." Baron nodded toward the chair closest to the man. "This is Otto Hoermann with Abwehr Military Intelligence Service. He asked to meet you." Baron's tone substituted "demanded" for "asked" as he sat at his paper-cluttered desk, arms crossed tight.

I didn't know who was more annoyed by the agent's presence, Baron or me.

"*Herr* Pepperman." Hoermann scooted a chair next to mine. The screech the legs made as they slid across the floor put an even more sour look on Baron's face. Hoermann didn't offer a handshake, nod, or even a loosening of his tight mouth. Nothing to indicate this was a friendly meeting. "I'd like to ask you a question. Do you mind?"

Did it matter? His condescending tone spiked my dislike for him.

Fist over his mouth, he coughed—a deep tobacco cough—and his suit stretched even more. Whiffs of sweat flooded the room. "I'll get right to the point. Do you have relatives in America?" He finally undid his jacket and let the bulge breathe.

I turned in my chair and faced him. "Why do I get the feeling you already know the answer?"

Baron straightened in his chair. "Hans."

Pressure built in my neck, and I loosened my tie. "Yes, *Herr* Hoermann, I have relatives in America."

Hoermann grinned, exposing his two front teeth. One slightly overlapped the other. "You seem upset by my question. Let me put you at ease. All new employees, especially those with tight security jobs, go through a background check by the Military Intelligence Service."

"Shouldn't you have done your investigation before I was hired?" I matched his arrogance.

Hoermann checked his watch. "The wheels of bureaucracy move slowly. Please forgive us. And you moved to Augsburg to work with Messerschmitt." He angled his head toward my boss. "I must catch a train to Munich. I'm sorry to have interrupted your day." The pompous *arsch* stood and pulled his pants above his girth. The dark stare he gave me with his snakelike eyes felt like fingers tightening around my neck. "The service will be in touch."

Despite the tightness in my throat, I returned the stare. If he wanted to play games, he picked the wrong person.

Hoermann shuffled toward the door, each step arduous and painful looking.

I leaned forward in my chair after he left. "What was that all about?"

Baron twirled a pencil between his fingers, another sign of his annoyance at the *schwein* Hoermann. He shook his head. "I suppose the intelligent services are cautious of everyone. Germany is years ahead of every other nation in fighter plane technology. Perhaps the government is concerned with other countries stealing our ideas."

"Is Germany preparing for war?"

"I don't know." Baron rubbed a hand across his mouth. "My hope is Germany wants to become strong so no nation will challenge us. As far as this meeting with Hoermann, I wouldn't be too concerned. They check out everyone — especially someone new to the industry." He smiled and tossed the pencil to the corner of his desk.

I didn't like Hoermann. Or that he'd dug into my personal life. Who cared if I had American relatives?

CHAPTER 13

der 16. Januar 1937
Augsburg, Germany

I PACKED MY PERSONAL BELONGINGS IN MAMA'S OLD TRUNK TO take back with me to the hotel. At the last minute, I tucked the picture of my cousin and me inside the Olympic jacket I had worn at the Opening Ceremonies the first time we met. Family is important. The jacket and my Olympic lapel boxing pen that I kept inside a wooden keepsake box will always remind me of what should have been mine – the gold medal...

The drive from Stuttgart back to Augsburg gave me plenty of time to think. Yesterday, the *Berliner Zeitung* ran a story about a Maybach executive selling truck engine designs to the Russians. Did Germany suspect me of spying? What did the Military Intelligence Service want with me? Why had they gone to the trouble of searching my background? I would never be a traitor to my country.

A Hotel Bauer doorman placed my trunk on a cart, barely managing to fit it and me into the elevator.

Just as the door was closing, Anna Beck walked into the hotel bar.

My heart ticked an unnatural beat. That woman did something to me I couldn't explain. Seeing Anna on

Saturday was unusual. I was tempted to motion for the doorman to come back and deliver the trunk to my room for me, but he'd already made it halfway across the lobby.

The elevator seemed to take forever. When I finally got to my floor, I shoved the trunk inside and headed right back down to the bar.

The tavern had few customers, especially for a weekend, and it was quieter than normal.

Anna sat at the end of the bar, facing away from me. Maybe we could have a normal conversation without raising our voices. "*Guten tag.* May I sit?"

She lowered a glass of red wine without looking at me. "Of course."

Her vanilla perfume reminded me of Bee Sting Cake—a dessert I would fight for.

Turning her head toward me, she slowly grinned. "I haven't seen you in a while."

Time stopped. At that moment, I was totally entrapped. I liked this woman, and I would fight for *her* too. I ran my index finger along the inside of my shirt collar to help catch the breath she'd just stolen away. "My boss called me back to the factory in Stuttgart."

Locking her eyes on mine, she squared herself on the bar stool, took a sip of wine, and swallowed. The look she gave me was undeniable. She was pleased to see me. "You are a busy engineer, back and forth between Augsburg and Stuttgart. What exactly do you do?"

I got the attention of the *barmann,* ordered a *bier*, and turned back to Anna. "Not much. I'm really just a glorified aircraft mechanic."

"You're being modest." She swirled her wine.

The *barmann* set my *bier* in front of me, and I took a generous swallow. "I analyze existing engines and see if improvements can be made."

A loud commotion came from the hotel lobby, men and women laughing and swearing.

"The wife of one of the staff had a baby." Anna dipped her head as though she didn't want to be here. "We're meeting here to celebrate."

I grinned and took another drink. "It sounds like the party started without you."

The loud crowd wound through the bar toward the back.

Anna narrowed her eyes at someone behind me, and I had a gut feeling I knew who.

"Well, look who we have here." Heinrich Adler, the crude Gestapo agent, confirmed my suspicion. "*Herr* Pepperman." He smacked a meaty hand down on my shoulder and squeezed. "Anna, did you invite this august engineer to our party?"

I grabbed his thick wrist and forced his hand off.

"No." Contempt hardened her tone. "I did not invite Hans to our party. He just happened to be here."

"Anna, you are so serious." Heinrich's laugh was at least as contemptuous as her tone. He flashed an insincere smile. "I would be glad if Hans joined us."

He moved in close, his face inches from mine. His breath smelled of peppermint Schnapps and bratwurst.

Anna slid off the stool, forcing herself between us. "Heinrich."

He reluctantly stepped back. "Of course. This should be a time of joy and celebration. Besides, I'd hate to bust my knuckles on such a pretty face."

I pushed my bar stool to the side, unbuttoned my coat, and braced myself.

Anna moved between us again. "Stop it, both of you. Heinrich, please join the others."

I looked to the back of the suddenly quiet bar.

All eyes were locked on Anna, Heinrich, and me.

Heinrich didn't say a word but wagged an index finger at me and turned and joined the others.

Anna exhaled and closed her eyes. When she opened them, her hand shook as she covered her mouth.

"What was that all about?" I kept my tone light. I wanted to let her know it was all over.

"Heinrich is jealous. He sees you as a threat for my affection."

Heinrich was right, but this wasn't the time to speak up. "Okay, go join the others and have a good evening."

She moved in close, setting her hand on my forearm. "Thank you," she whispered, "for not causing a scene."

The look in her eyes told me all I needed to know. She returned some of the feelings I had for her.

I watched as she walked to the party, hoping she'd turn around, but that didn't happen. I sat at the bar and waited. Maybe she would join me later.

After an hour, I knew she wouldn't.

The more I drank, the more I wanted to be with her. I went to the lavatory. After I'd finished and washed and dried my hands, I headed out the door.

Heinrich and two other men approached me. One man's pathetically sparse mustache caught my attention. He reminded me of a teenager struggling to grow his first facial hair.

They said nothing as they blocked me from leaving.

"You're in my way." I sensed this was not going to go well.

"I'm going to bust you up, Pepperman." Heinrich sniffed and spat on the floor, as though that would get rid of the bad taste he had for me.

I couldn't help but grin on the inside. "You don't know what you're getting into, Heinrich."

He pounded his fist into his palm. "You don't know what you're getting into. I was the heavyweight intramural boxing champion at my university."

Another tough guy. I shook my head. "Really, don't do this."

That seemed to embolden the poor fool. He put his fists next to his face and bounced up and down with the grace of a cartoon kangaroo.

If only he could see how silly he looked.

There was no way out for me. When he took his fighting stance, I had to defend myself, and it wasn't going to end well for Gestapo boy. I threw a straight, right cross, the same right cross I'd thrown a million times in the ring. My knockout punch. My fist landed square on his mouth.

Teeth popped like splintered ice. His legs buckled. And he fell back against the lavatory door and wilted to the floor, out cold.

I looked at his friends.

They stared at their crumpled, helpless comrade who'd pissed all over himself.

My torn knuckles dripped blood. I used my handkerchief to stop the flow. I pointed at the two men. "Who's next?"

Both backed away.

I dragged Heinrich by his tie to the urinal to clear the doorway. Then I left the lavatory and headed out of the bar.

"Halt." A voice came from behind me

The chilling command startled me, and I slowly turned.

Two guns were pointed at my chest.

CHAPTER 14

der 18. Januar 1937
Augsburg, Germany

I SPENT FRIDAY NIGHT THROUGH SUNDAY AFTERNOON IN *Augsburg's city jail. The bier vomit and strong smell of urine – I am sorry to say I added to the pungent puddles on the floor – were almost more than I could take.*

Several fights broke out. The guards never bothered to show up, even when one man was beaten so badly I thought he might die. And the food – if you could call the mold-speckled dried pumpernickel and cold, watered-down oxtail soup served once a day food – made me gag. I did not know inhumanity like this existed…

Monday morning Messerschmitt called me to his office.

Slow and ponderous, each step down the painted concrete hall was painful. My gut twisted like fresh-baked pretzels. At best, I expected to be sent back to Stuttgart. At worst, fired. Adjusting my coat, I entered his large wood-paneled office. "*Danke* for posting my bail. I—"

Messerschmitt held up a hand, cutting me off with a look that said spare me the details, and gestured to the green leather chair across from his paperless desk. A stark contrast from the clutter that had been there before.

As I sat, he interlocked his fingers and stared at me.

I didn't know what to say, so I just stared back, focusing on his bushy, black eyebrows.

After too many loud ticks of his antique *Junghans* wall clock, he dropped his hands and angled his head. "I know why you were arrested."

"*Herr* Messerschmitt—"

"You made a colossal mistake." His tone was as dry as an ancient riverbed. "Don't mess with the Gestapo. In order to free you, I had to assure them many times over that you are vital to the defense of Germany. They will be watching every move you make. You step out of line again, and I won't be able to help you."

"Do you want to know—?"

"The less I know the better."

"May I ask how you found out I was in jail?"

Messerschmitt leaned back, resting his forearms on his chair. "A lady by the name of Anna Beck called me. Is this young lady special?" His eyebrows twitched. He propped one elbow on his desk to set a hand on his cheek, as though he was perturbed with the entire matter.

"She is." The catch in my throat attested to that truth.

"Was she with you the night of the incident?"

"Yes."

Messerschmitt scratched his temple. "I know the *brutaler* you knocked out. He deserved it, I'm sure." He slouched in his chair, interlocking his fingers and resting them on his stomach.

I gave him a casual nod. "Anything else?" I wanted out of his sight before he changed his mind and actually did send me back to Stuttgart.

"There is one more thing."

I held my breath. He was going to fire me. How could I talk him out of it?

"If you receive a dental bill from the *dummkoph*, bring it to me." He gestured to the door in dismissal.

I inhaled and relaxed. Nodding, I got up from the chair and went to my office.

As soon as 5:00 p.m. arrived, I caught the train to the Hotel Bauer hoping to see Anna before she left work.

She wasn't in the bar or her office, so I hurried to my room to get her phone number. I went to the lobby pay phone and called her apartment.

"Anna Beck, *guten tag.*"

"Anna, this is Hans." My high-pitched voice gave away that I was a little too excited.

"Hans." Her soft tone peaked with emotion.

"I tried to catch you at the hotel. I wanted to thank you for calling Messerschmitt to get me out of jail."

"Of course." Music was playing in the background. "I felt it was my fault you were arrested in the first place."

"Nonsense, you weren't to blame for anything." I paused, nervously fingering the phone cord. "Would you like to have dinner after work tomorrow?"

She cleared her throat. "I would like that very much."

"*Gut. Gut.*" If words could dance, mine would be doing the polka.

Thinking about our dinner, I didn't sleep much. The next morning while shaving, I was humming the

American song *One O'Clock Jump* when a loud knock interrupted me. After wiping the shaving cream off with a towel, I slipped on my trousers and went to the door.

Two men — one tall and skinny, the other short and plump — showed their Gestapo badges. "Are you Hans Pepperman?"

I flipped the towel over my bare shoulder. "Yes. What's this about?" My voice gave away my anxiety.

One of the men wore a smirk. He cocked his head to one side. "We want to talk to you about the murder of Heinrich Adler."

I felt my jaw drop. I took the towel from my shoulder and patted my face. My pulse raced. I looked at the condescending agent, the one with the twisted smile. "What? Murder? Why do you want to talk with me? Am I under arrest?"

He raised his head, looking at me over his long, pointed nose. "*Nein.*"

Because of Messerschmitt's warning, I dressed and went with them to their headquarters on the second floor of the hotel. Three full hotel rooms had been made into one big office, desks jammed close to each other. The smell of stale coffee and spent cigarette smoke made me cough.

We passed a desk with Heinrich Adler's name plate. He actually had a framed picture of a stripper performing a dance in full sight. Half-filled paper coffee cups with cigarette butts floating in them littered the rest of the desk. Why hadn't anyone cleaned up his mess?

The creep was a blockhead, but I didn't want him dead. And now I wished I hadn't beaten him up.

The men took me to Fritz Schiffter, a portly, squat man who wore tiny round glasses that were too small for his large head. His square jawline and little, straight mouth reminded me of a boar hog.

He pointed to a chair in front of his metal desk. "Did you know Heinrich Adler?" He already knew the answer. But the question was part of a game I wasn't sure I'd be any good at playing.

"We had a fight. I knocked out his front teeth. Then it was over." I smiled and tried to loosen up. "Come on, people."

Adjusting his glasses, the hog-jowled agent leaned over his desk. "Do not make light with your answers." His tone was butcher-knife sharp.

I needed to be careful and not antagonize these people.

Schiffter leaned back in his chair. He picked up a file, opened it, and began to read. "Heinrich Rudolph Adler was found in the Lach River, Monday, *der 18 Januar*, at 8:42 a.m., nude with his throat slashed. He had been castrated."

Mouth dry, I leaned back in my chair. I blinked several times. Was I dreaming? Surely the Gestapo didn't believe I could do such a thing.

Schiffter slowly closed the file. "Are you familiar with the brothel located two miles from the city limits on the Lach River?"

I shook my head. "*Nein.*" I wanted to point out that if Adler had been found nude near a brothel, wouldn't that be the place to look for the killer? But I gripped the arms of the chair and kept quiet.

Schiffter removed his glasses and tapped them on Adler's file. "Do not leave Augsburg. You are not a suspect yet, but you are a person of interest. We are looking very closely at you — very closely." Like he was shooing me from his presence, he motioned for me to leave with the back of his hand

Happy to go, I pushed away from his desk.

CHAPTER 15

der 22. Januar 1937
Augsburg, Germany

THE GESTAPO HAS NOTHING ON ME CONCERNING ADLER'S *death because there is nothing. So, why am I a person of interest? That question annoys me more than it puzzles me. I would rather focus on Anna. She called me at work Tuesday and changed our dinner date to Friday, tonight. I cannot wait…*

It was easier to catch the trolley from the Bauer Hotel and go directly to *Fuggerei* Public Housing. Besides, driving my old car was an embarrassment.

Arriving at Anna's apartment at 6:05 p.m., I quickly found number 11 and knocked. My knuckles stung against the cold, heavy door. I heard footsteps.

The latch clanked, and Anna opened the door. She wore a long-sleeved gold blouse with a large bow that settled just under her chin. The blouse was tucked neatly into a tight, straight black skirt emphasizing her small waist. Wavy brown hair framed her rosy cheeks.

I stepped inside, mesmerized. "You look beautiful."

She curtsied. "*Dankeschön*, kind sir." Handing me her beige wool coat, she turned her back. "Will you help me?"

"Of course." I held the coat, and she slipped her arms into the sleeves. Her rose fragrance engulfed me. The temptation to kiss her neck pulled me closer, but I resisted. A bit too much, too early. But maybe later. For now, I was proud to be her escort for the evening.

As we left the *Fuggerei*, large flakes of snow floated past the streetlights, and Anna stuck out her hand. The ice crystals piled up like bits of confectionery sugar and melted in the warmth of her palm. She looked up at me — a strong woman with the eyes of an innocent young girl.

The complex contradictions that were Anna never ceased to amaze me.

As the trolley pulled up, she locked her arm around mine. "I have a special place tonight. The Ratskeller in the basement of Augsburg's town hall is my favorite restaurant. The Bavarian cuisine is excellent. Does that sound good to you?"

We could eat dried beef in the basement of a *bier* hall, and I wouldn't care, but all I said was, "I'm fond of Bavarian food."

The short trip to the restaurant gave us little time to talk. Weekend crowds filled the busy area. Women clutched the collars of their coats to keep the snow out, and the men sank their hands into their pockets.

Anna still had her arm linked with mine. "I'm glad I made reservations. You can thank me later." Her soft laughter had a hint of playfulness.

I loved that laughter most about her. I was falling for this woman too fast.

A concierge dressed in a heavy blue overcoat and military hat opened the door for us, and we walked down a short flight of stairs to the restaurant.

Anna unbuttoned her jacket and flicked a few of the snowflakes off the sleeve before we checked our coats.

Heavy ornate wooden beams crisscrossing the ceiling accentuated the Gothic style interior. The room had the ambiance of a medieval banquet hall.

"*Guten abend*." A man in a black tuxedo greeted us. "Do you have a reservation, Miss Beck?"

The host knew her name. She must come here often. I hoped it wasn't with other men. My heart sank.

"*Herr* Pepperman, party of two," Anna said.

The tall, blond host flipped the pages of the reservation book. "Ah, yes. 6:45. Please follow me. We have your favorite table ready." He took us to a table covered with a white linen cloth in the back corner near a fireplace. One lighted candle flicked a shadow on the wall.

The host pulled out the high-backed mahogany chair with a plush red velvet cushion and seated Anna, fluffed her napkin, and gestured to my seat. He nodded to another man standing quietly behind him. "This is Frederick, your waiter."

Frederick was at least 6' 3" with broad shoulders. The smile he gave us was genuine — unlike the smiles some waiters flashed that quickly faded.

"How's your wife?" Anna touched his forearm. "And your lovely little girls?"

"They're fine, Miss Beck. Thank you for asking." He bent at the waist, then straightened and handed us menus.

Anna ordered a glass of *Liebfraumilch*. I didn't have a taste for the tannic red wine, but my usual *bier* didn't seem right for tonight. Schnapps was my next choice.

When the waiter brought our drinks, Anna leaned over her menu. "Hans, do you mind if I order for us?"

"Go ahead." Her request caught me off guard, but with Anna that seemed to happen a lot. Most women would let the man order, but she was not a typical woman. And I liked that about her.

"For an appetizer, we'd like one pretzel, not too much salt. One white sausage and sweet mustard. For the main course, pork tenderloin with wine sauce, spaetzle dumplings and shallots for each of us."

Frederick wrote down our order. "Anything else, Madam."

"*Nein.*"

I noticed his gigantic hands with long fingers when we handed him the menus.

I took a sip of my drink.

Anna's eyes narrowed, and her head tipped to one side. "What happened to that knuckle on your right hand? It's huge."

I set the drink down and rubbed the joint. "I broke my hand during a training session. I'm a boxer." I chuckled. "I was a boxer."

"You boxed professionally?"

"*Nein.* The Olympic team. The break happened a week before the games started in August. My replacement won the gold medal."

"Which could have been yours?" She studied my hand.

"Perhaps."

Anna tipped her glass, then lowered it. "That's a shame. I'm so sorry. I'm a downhill racer who also had Olympic dreams. I broke my ankle during the first run in Garmish last February."

Remarkable. Two athletes who lost out on Olympic dreams. Fate had brought us together. I just knew it. "Sorry for your misfortune. I know the disappointment." I nodded, lifted my glass, and we toasted.

Not being used to strong alcohol, I quickly felt the effects of the clear liqueur. But it relaxed me enough to savor the special evening even more with this extraordinary lady.

A man at another table across the room next to the wine rack looked our way. I'd never seen him before, but there was something about him. Maybe he was looking at Anna. Men seemed to appreciate her, and I didn't blame them.

When Frederick set the large pretzel and the thick, white sausage between us, the meat was more round than long.

Anna pinched off a piece of bread and grinned. "Germans do it with big sausages."

I almost choked and had to set down my drink.

Her expression never changed as she tore off another piece of pretzel and dipped the bread into the sweet mustard. However, she did let out the tiniest hint of a chuckle as if she knew exactly what she was doing.

I followed with a laugh that drew the attention of those sitting around us.

The smell of the pork tenderloin reminded me of a meal served at an Olympic banquet, but the wine sauce added to the flavor.

Anna sipped on her fourth glass of wine. "Ah, I almost forgot. The Bee Sting Cake is the best. You must try it."

I puffed my cheeks and patted my stomach. "*Nein*, I'm too full, even though it's my favorite. I couldn't possibly…"

"Then we will share a slice." Her soft whisper sealed the request.

I motioned to Frederick. "One slice of Bee Sting Cake, a small slice, and two forks."

Occasionally Anna's eyes locked with mine as we ate. This had been an enjoyable night, and I hoped it wouldn't end too soon. When the food and drink were gone, I paid Frederick. Anna and I gathered our coats, and we headed back up the stairs. I pushed open the door.

Several inches of snow covered the sidewalk. The flakes were big and gently cascaded back and forth to the ground, bringing a clean freshness to the night air.

The trolley arrived. Our timing was perfect. The evening had passed quickly, and the Schnapps still buzzed in my head. I felt good as we clasped hands and walked to Anna's apartment. The fresh fallen snow crunched under our feet. Neither of us talked as she opened her purse and pulled out her key to unlock the door.

Anna paused, pushed the door, and stepped inside. She turned. Her eyes caught and held mine. There were no words, just a long, deep stare. Then she grabbed my tie, slowly pulled me inside, and closed the door.

She'd taken charge at the restaurant. The rest of the night was no different.

CHAPTER 16

der 23. Januar 1937
Augsburg, Germany

LAST NIGHT WITH ANNA? REMARKABLE. WHAT IS IT ABOUT HER
that just seems to shift something inside me every time we are
together? Not sure whether it is her soft giggle, her strong
character, or her unwavering self-confidence that does me in,
but I am sure all of her leaves me spellbound. Anna is every-
thing I have ever wanted in a woman…

Closing my journal, I glanced at my watch. 2:20 p.m.
Time for Bavarian *Volksmusik* in the hotel bar. I put on
my sweater and adjusted the collar of my shirt. Before I
could pull open the door, someone knocked.

Anna perhaps? A little excitement kicked up in my
chest, but quickly disappeared when I opened the door
to two men. Standing shoulder to shoulder, both wore
black overcoats and Wyeth wool hats in a way that was
reminiscent of gangsters in American movies.

"Hans Pepperman?" The man on the left had a bulbous nose. His nostrils flexed with each word.

I nodded.

"Come with us." The other man, smaller with jug-han-
dled ears, stepped forward as if to grab my arm. "We
have questions."

I felt another kick in my chest, and there was nothing exciting about it. I didn't care for his threatening tone or the way his dark eyes locked on mine. I cleared my throat. "Questions about what?" I swallowed hard, my pulse ticking up several notches.

Large Nose pulled the other man back. "*Herr* Pepperman. We're with the Abwehr Military Intelligence."

If he was trying to calm me with his slow, deep voice, it wasn't working. "We just want to ask you a few questions," he said. "Please come with us."

Dealing with Gestapo and the Military Intelligence had first been a nuisance. Now I was getting a little concerned by their attention. As a patriot, I loved my country, but I would never support a racist Nazi Party. I didn't think that was what they wanted to hear. "Do I have a choice?"

"No." The smaller man methodically shook his head. The way his teeth gleamed through his crooked smile reminded me of a badger.

Large Nose stepped back to give me room to come into the hall.

Reluctantly, I stepped out and locked my door. "Who's asking these questions and where?"

"Otto Hoermann." He gestured toward the elevator. "Gestapo office. Here in the Bauer Hotel. It's on the—"

"Second floor." Hoermann. The man with the bad body odor in Baron's office. I could have done without another meeting with him.

When I hesitated, the two Abwher officers each grabbed one of my upper arms and marched me to the elevator. "I told you it was not a choice." The smaller one had a short-man complex.

Most of my annoyance turned to tension, then progressed to a mound of anger. What did Hoermann want? I had nothing of interest for him. So what made him think I did? I wondered if working for Daimler had been a good idea. This wasn't what I'd expected. I just wanted to go to work every day and do the job I was trained to do.

On the second floor, a deep cigarette cough came from the Gestapo room. The same cough I'd heard in Baron's office.

The agents opened the door and led me inside.

My gaze went straight to the once-cluttered desk of Heinrich Adler. Today, it appeared clean and strangely unoccupied and gave me the same angry feeling I'd had each time Adler had looked at Anna in a provocative, ogling way. He'd been an uncouth brute.

That raspy cough pulled my gaze to the back of the room. Just like last time, the stench of stale cigarette smoke and burnt coffee mixed with food turned my stomach.

The small man gave me a push toward Hoermann.

"He doesn't like waiting." Definitely an obnoxious swine.

Hoermann's short, bulky frame, oily black hair, and thick-blocked mustache were exactly the same as I'd remembered.

As I moved closer, the smell of sweat combined with the smoke and coffee almost made me gag.

"Ah, *Herr* Pepperman." He stood from behind the metal desk, and the chair seemed to moan as if relieved from the loss of his bulk. "How good to see you again. Please, have a seat."

His phony pretense only heightened my tension. There was no telling what these fanatics would try to pin on me. I pulled a flimsy wooden chair away from the desk and sat down hard. "What's this all about, Hoermann?" I tried to sound as if I didn't care, but I don't think it worked.

He popped the last button on his suit jacket, releasing a bulge of jammed-up belly fat and sat. "Only a few questions. This is Saturday, and I know you want to enjoy your day off. You told me in Stuttgart that you have relatives in America. Is that correct?"

"Yes." I rested my elbows on the chair arms and interlocked my fingers, mostly to keep them from shaking.

"What do you know about those relatives?" He made it sound like he knew more than I did.

Why did I feel that no matter what I said, he wouldn't be appeased? I drew in a deep breath and exhaled. "My father's brother Wilhelm and Wilhelm's son Patrick came to Germany to see me box in the Olympics. That was the first time I'd ever met them." I stuck with the truth. I had nothing to hide. But Hoermann's stare still made me feel as if I did.

"Do you know what Wilhelm does for a living?" He went very still in his chair, like a tiger ready to pounce.

"He's a businessman. An accountant in Washington, DC." Again, the truth.

"An accountant for the federal government?"

I sensed he was baiting me, leading me somewhere I didn't want to go. I gripped the arms of my chair. "I don't know." Tension leaked out in my voice in the form of irritation.

Hoermann finally moved. Everything about him—his crossed arms, his soft persuading tone, his piercing eyes—showed he enjoyed his role of power. "Are you upset with my questions, *Herr* Pepperman?"

I'd already given myself away, so I couldn't lie. "Yes, I'm upset." But I could deflect. "Your henchmen drag me in here on the weekend. You ask me about relatives I barely know. You don't even offer me a cup of coffee." Not that I'd drink that sludge. "Of course, I'm upset. What's your point?"

Hoermann pounded on the desk—a short, staccato sound—so hard his knuckles went white. "My point, sir?" He paused dramatically as if he were on stage and flashed me a hideous smile. "My point is… that your Uncle Wilhelm is a spy."

His heavy emphasis on the word spy sent chills through my core. Hoermann might as well have taken a dagger and carved out my heart. Calling Uncle Wilhelm a spy was like calling a saint a sinner. Pure nonsense.

Hoermann leaned back in his chair and briefly put his hand over his mouth. "Herr Pepperman, things are a little tense. Would you mind taking a walk with me outside to clear the air?"

The invitation was unusual, and I sensed him pulling back a bit. I had no idea why, but anything I could do to get these people to leave me alone was worth a try. "I have to get my coat."

Hoermann lifted his arm and sniffed his armpit. "Bromhidrosis." He looked at me, obvious sadness in his eyes.

I stood. "Excuse me?"

"Overactive sweat glands." He walked to the coat rack, his steps arduous and painful to watch. He looked at the two men who had met me at my door and gave a flippant motion with his hand. "Thank you. I won't need you the rest of the day. You are dismissed."

I hurried to my room, grabbed my coat, and met Hoermann in the lobby. As we walked outside, the sun broke through the low-hanging clouds, slowing down the snowstorm.

Maintenance men shoveled the sidewalks while the north wind snapped at my neck, and I wished I'd brought my scarf.

Hoermann's hat was pulled down almost covering his ears, and his long overcoat scraped the ground. He looked like a stuffed bear dressed in clothes. He shifted weight from one foot to the other trying to stay warm. "Let's go to the south side of the hotel to get out of the wind. I have some things to say, and I want no one to hear."

The short walk gave some relief from the freezing winter blast.

Hoermann tightened the scarf around his neck and looked both ways. "May I call you Hans?"

"Of course."

"We've known about your Uncle Wilhelm for some time. I was shocked when we spotted you with him at the Olympics. Because of your education and your job at Daimler-Benz, the military intelligence considered you a possible spy as well."

"Me, a spy? That's insane. I—"

Hoermann cut me off with a raised hand. "Do not worry. I've thoroughly vetted you. I know about your amateur boxing, your family in Hamburg. I even know where you spent last night."

Verdammt. These people knew everything about my life for the past six months.

Hoermann placed a calming hand on my shoulder. "I don't believe you are involved in espionage against our country. But the Gestapo is not sure. Foreign intelligence is somehow getting information on Germany's fighter plane development." He paused and looked long and hard at me.

Where was this conversation going? What was he up to?

Hoermann cupped his hands over his mouth and blew. "I've convinced my superiors of your loyalty to the Fatherland and received permission for you to help us find out who's leaking information to our enemies. Would you be willing to help us?"

CHAPTER 17

der 24. Januar 1937
Augsburg, Germany

YESTERDAY'S CONVERSATION WITH HOERMANN BLITZED MY
jumbled mind. My loyalty to Germany is undeniable. I want
to help my country. Yet I despise their growing hatred of
the Jews. The night in Braunschweig last October when the
Jewish shopkeeper was bullied highlights their bigotry. I want
no part of anyone affiliated with the Nazis.

Is there a way to accept Hoermann's offer without sacrificing my principles? He had called himself a patriot, not a
true member of the Party. But those are just words. If I agree
to help, can I trust him? If I refuse to help, what will happen
to me? And what about the Gestapo? They still think I had
something to do with Heinrich Adler's death...

Three short taps came from the other side of my door.

Who could be visiting on a Sunday afternoon? I put
my journal in the bedside table drawer, slipped on my
shirt, and went to see.

Anna, another lady, and Ernst Fischer from work
were standing there with smiles plastered on their faces.

My heavy heart lightened. Anna's face kicked my
pulse into overdrive, and I smiled at her.

"Well, aren't you going to ask us in?" she said.

I hastily buttoned my shirt and stepped back. "Of course."

Anna walked into the room, then turned back toward the woman. "Hans, this is my friend, Heidi Gennette Graf. We live in the same complex."

A little bit shorter than Anna, Heidi was just as beautiful with soft, brown eyes and a warm smile.

"And you know Ernst," Anna said.

Ernst took Heidi's hand and gently moved her inside.

Puzzled, I scratched my temple. They were a couple? Ernst and Heidi didn't seem to match, what with her beauty and his... well... slumped shoulders, thinning hair, and thick glasses.

Anna placed a friendly hand on Ernst's shoulder. "Ernst has been a friend of mine for several years. I didn't know you worked with him until today when he came by to see Heidi."

Anna had wanted to see me today. At least I hoped so. That made me happy.

"Come with us to a *kaffee* shop near the hotel." She tugged on my arm.

Yesterday's storm had completely moved on. The sidewalk was wet but clean of snow, and the sun reflected off a window across the street.

Krause's Kaffee Haus was a popular place for the working class in this area. Several times I'd been there for their blueberry *kaffee* cake.

I opened the door.

Anna stepped in first. She motioned to the waiter to seat us near the window. "Four *kaffees* with rum and sugar topped with whipped cream."

"No *kaffee* for me," I said as we followed the man. "Just *kaffee* cake."

"The same for me." Ernst sheepishly raised his hand and ducked his chin as though he didn't want to offend Anna. "Just cake."

Anna arched her eyebrows. "Well," she said, "let's all have *kaffee* cake and no *kaffee*."

The waiter fumbled to get his pad and pen out of his pocket, either flustered by the changes or more likely by Anna. "We have apple or blueberry."

"Blueberry with vanilla ice cream for me." I pulled a chair from the table and seated Anna to my right.

Everyone else ordered as Ernst seated Heidi next to me and took his chair at the square, glossy, oak table.

The paneled walls in the restaurant, decorated with medieval family crests and flickering lamps, created an ambiance that felt more like a fine restaurant. The decor was a bit much for a *kaffee* house.

Heidi moved her purse from her lap to the floor. "Hans, Ernst said you are a mechanical engineer. That's impressive. Can you tell me what you do?"

"I help build and design aircraft engines."

"Ah." Her eyes shimmered and her tone lifted. "Ernst builds the airplane, and you build the engines."

I nodded. "That's about it."

The waiter set the cake in front of me. The smell took me back to my childhood and the blueberry muffins my grandmother always had waiting for me after school. I took a bite. Still not as good as Grandma's. Probably because there wasn't any cinnamon streusel on the top or hot butter cascading down the sides to pool on the plate.

Anna asked Ernst a question, but I wasn't paying attention.

Heidi adjusted her skirt. "The dynamics of the internal combustion engine and how the ignition and the combustion of the fuel occur are fascinating."

I sat back in my chair. "Yes, fascinating is a good way to describe it." I didn't want to get into a protracted discussion about the intricacies of the secret BF 109. I changed the subject. "What do you do for a living?"

She scooted her chair closer to the table. "I'm an English translator for the Augsburg newspaper."

She deciphered English and had some proficiency in mechanical engineering. That was a little odd. "I didn't realize newspapers needed English translators."

"The Augsburg newspaper receives teletyped articles from New York and London daily," Heidi said. "I translate the news into German, then pass the information to government officials."

My chest tightened until it felt like I'd been strapped to a table, the same feeling I'd had yesterday when talking to Hoermann. Who in the government wanted to know what was going on in America and England? And why?

CHAPTER 18

der 25. Januar 1937
Augsburg, Germany

I AM DREADING TODAY, NOT BECAUSE OF MY JOB, BUT BECAUSE I agreed to meet Hoermann tonight at seven. Even if I were not hesitant about helping the Abwehr Military Intelligence uncover leaks within the aircraft industry, how would I do it? I am not trained in espionage. And trusting Hoermann means putting my life in jeopardy...

Outside the Bauer, the streetlights cast an eerie glow, and howling wind whipped snowflakes into a frenzy. Waiting in the lobby, I caught my own reflection in the large glass window. My anxious eyes told the truth. Spying was not in my blood.

A black Mercedes drove by. Hoermann's pumpkin-shaped head topped with a black hat gave him away as the driver. He turned the corner and disappeared.

Apprehensive about the storm that had started midafternoon, I jammed both hands into the pockets of my coat and pushed through the revolving door with my shoulder. A blast of bitter cold wind slammed against my chest. Maybe an omen warning me to turn around and go back inside? I joined Hoermann at the side of the building as we had planned.

Ignoring the tight burn building in my chest, I concentrated on the screeching windshield wipers as they struggled to clear the heavy snow off the front window. As I opened the passenger side door, a glob of snow fell off the roof onto the seat. I brushed it off and slid in.

Hoermann pulled the glove off his right hand and greeted me with a handshake.

His strong grip and the cold weather caused a familiar ache in my knuckle, and I flexed my fingers. Unlike spying, boxing was up front and clear cut, the task simple — outsmart and defeat the man in front of you.

"*Guten tag, Herr* Pepperman. Thank you for meeting me tonight." His friendly tone took some of the burn out of my chest. "This weather." He shook his head. "I'm sorry to bring you out into this miserable mess."

I scrunched my shoulders. "It's *Januar* in Bavaria. What can we expect?"

Hoermann checked the traffic and pulled back onto the street. The heater and fan were on full blast, his body odor exacerbated by both.

I unbuttoned my coat, wanting to pinch my nostrils. "Could you lower the temperature and turn down the fan?"

"Of course." He adjusted the controls. "I'll get right to the point. Have you had enough time to consider helping protect our government from foreign entities?"

"I've been thinking about your offer all weekend." My stomach felt like I'd been gut punched. "I want to protect my country, but I don't feel qualified. I have no training in this field."

Hoermann slowed down to stop at a traffic light, his expression as even as the way he braked the car. "All I'd like for you to do is be on alert. If someone asks about your job and the questions appear to be too technical, be suspicious."

The light changed, and he pulled through the intersection. "The intelligence service wants you to be our eyes and ears."

If that were true, why was the knot in my stomach growing big enough to meet the burn in my chest? I looked at him, shaking my head. "Is that all? That sounds too simple."

Hoermann sniffed, rubbed his nose, and looked straight ahead. "If we suspect someone ourselves, we'll ask you to get to know him and find out as much as you can."

"And what if his comrades suspect me?"

Hoermann glanced at me with a look that froze my heart. "They will torture and kill you."

His straightforward words rattled in my skull. It's not that I hadn't suspected such treatment but hearing him say it made it all too real. I blew out a breath and turned toward him. "That's more than just being your eyes and ears. You're asking me to be—and take all the risks of—a counterintelligence agent." I wiped a jittery hand across my mouth and cleared my throat.

He nodded.

"So why would I put my life on the line for a group of fanatical politicians I hate?" I couldn't keep the venom out of my tone.

"The same reason I do. For the love of my country." Hoermann drove back to the side of the Bauer Hotel and stopped the car. "I know this is hard for you, but a lot is at stake."

"If I agree to help, will you and the military intelligence have my back? I won't do this unless you support me one hundred percent."

"You can trust me. I'll support you with every resource we have." There was a sincere quality in Hoermann's face I hadn't seen before.

I felt I could trust him. But deep down, I knew my life would be expendable if I got caught.

"Will you help us?" he asked again.

How had I even gotten into this situation? Angry at myself for accepting his offer and angry at him for asking, I gave a reluctant nod. Buttoning my coat, I stepped from the car.

A man leaving the hotel caught my attention. His scarf covered his neck and wrapped tight around his mouth, and his red stocking cap was pulled to his eyebrows. He crossed the street, looked back in my direction, but kept walking. His movements looked familiar, but I couldn't see his face.

CHAPTER 19

der 26. Januar 1937
Augsburg, Germany

SLEEP DID NOT COME EASY LAST NIGHT. AGREEING TO WORK with Hoermann still makes my stomach churn. If I suspect someone of stealing secrets about our fighter planes, I will do the minimum. Then Hoermann will have to follow up…

At 7:20 a.m., there was no time for breakfast and barely enough time to catch the train to Bavarian Aircraft Works. Slipping on my overcoat, I headed out the door and reached the elevator just as it opened.

Anna stood there. Her red coat and matching beret with a black-and-white checked bow jumpstarted my lethargic heart. But it was her smile as she stepped out of the elevator that sent me into orbit.

"*Guten morgen,* Anna." I smiled back, tipping an imaginary hat. A stupid gesture, I know, but I couldn't help myself.

She set her hand on my forearm and gave a light stroke. "I'm glad I saw you. I'd planned on calling today to see if you wanted to meet Heidi and me in the hotel bar for a drink after work." She lowered her chin.

The only way I wouldn't show up would be if I were in a coffin. "Of course. Around 6:00?"

She slowly drew her hand down my arm and squeezed my hand. "Perfect." She turned and walked down the hall.

The sway of her hips? Now that was perfect. I watched her until she disappeared inside her office, wasting time I didn't really have.

Messerschmitt wanted to see me before my workday started. Last week, he'd hinted I could be assigned to Augsburg if Daimler-Benz would allow it.

Being the only fighter plane engine specialist at the airframe facility could be good for my career. My progress with the oil pump and the roller bearing issue was falling into place. Replacing the roller bearing with a journal bearing still needed more testing.

I hurried to catch the next train, fighting the frigid wind. I rubbed my hands together to get warm, the train not usually this cold.

At work, the guard at the gate motioned me in through the checkpoint, barely glancing at my credentials. The cold wind must be getting to him, too.

The hallway to Messerschmitt's office was jammed with people, usual for this time of day. The chatter was everything from sports to politics.

Messerschmitt's secretary, Miss Baigelman, greeted me with a Marlene Dietrich smile, dreamy eyes, and parted lips. "*Herr* Pepperman, is there anything I can do for you?"

Her coy manner wasn't a surprise. She'd greeted me before with flirtatious words and gestures. I didn't mind. "*Nein*, thank you. I just need to talk with *Herr* Messerschmitt."

"He's waiting for you." She pointed to his door, still beaming that bedroom smile.

A fog of cigarette smoke welcomed me — the haze so thick you could drive a nail through it.

"Hans, have a seat." His happy tone seemed a good omen. "Great news from Daimler. Baron said you can stay here a while longer." He jammed his already full ashtray with one more partially smoked tobacco stick.

I pulled a chair back from his desk and sat. "How long is a while longer?"

He moved the stinking ashtray to the corner of his desk and rolled out a blueprint. "I didn't ask. If I could have my way, you'd be here permanently."

That was a welcome compliment from a man not prone to praise. To the casual observer, Messerschmitt appeared an ordinary, balding, middle-aged man with no muscle tone who smoked too much. To me, he was an aeronautical genius.

He looked at the blueprint, pulled out another cigarette from the mostly empty pack, and lit up. He took a deep drag and exhaled a raincloud of smoke in my direction. "How's the work on the oil pump going?"

I blew a puff of air upward to rid my nose of the suffocating smell. "I'm making progress."

"*Gut.* Glad you are with us, Pepperman." Short and to the point. A typical response from Willy Messerschmitt.

The day passed quickly. Anxious to see Anna, I left as soon as I could. Outside, I saw Ernst Fischer getting into his car. "Ernst, wait up." I caught up to him before he shut his door.

"Anna and Heidi will be at the Bauer for a drink. Are you coming?"

"*Nein*. I'm having some design issues on the new medium range bomber." He shut the door.

Not at all the friendly guy from the other night, he must've had a hell of a bad day. Work did that sometimes. I shrugged at his standoffish behavior. Seeing Anna was more important than a drink with a coworker.

The train was late pulling into the station close to the hotel. I hoped Anna and Heidi hadn't given up on me.

The cold temperatures had kept most of the snow from melting, but there were some slush puddles in the road to navigate. One slippery spot almost caused me to lose my balance.

A young man across the way wasn't as fortunate. He lost his footing, and the first thing that hit the ground was his derriere. He hopped up quickly and brushed himself off.

Stomping my ice-laden shoes before entering the hotel lobby, I sent bits of brownish water splattering against the revolving door.

Laughter came from the bar, louder than usual for a workday.

I stepped into the room.

Anna waved to get my attention. She and Heidi sat at a small round table near the middle of the lounge. Anna's eyes were glued to mine.

A warm feeling filled my chest. She was becoming more and more special to me. I walked toward her.

A man seated at the bar turned his stool and stuck out his leg in front of me. "Pepperman, nice to see you again." His tone was sarcastic and filled with hate.

I recognized the Gestapo agent from the night Adler and I had fought in the lavatory of this bar. I remembered his sparse black mustache. He was one of those guys who tried desperately to grow facial hair but was woefully inadequate.

"Do you remember me?" His fake grin exposed the worst mouth of crooked teeth I'd ever seen.

I looked down at his leg, then up to his face. "What do you want?"

"Nothing. Just wanted to say hello." He took a big drink of his *bier* and set it back on the bar.

What was he doing? I'd seen him a few other times in the lounge, and he'd never acknowledged I was even in the room. Making direct eye contact, I wasn't about to let him bully me. "Is there anything else you want to say?"

He shook his head. "Why the tone? Why are you so sensitive?"

I tapped him on the chest, not hard but stern enough to let him know I wouldn't put up with his *scheisse*. "Don't ever put your leg out in front of me again."

He sat back in his chair, resting his elbows on the bar. "And if I do?"

"I'll rearrange all those crooked teeth."

He laughed and turned back to face the bar.

When I reached Anna and Heidi, I could tell by the look on Anna's face she'd witnessed the conversation. "*Guten abend*, ladies." I sat across from her.

"What was that all about?" she asked. "I saw you put a finger in the Gestapo agent's chest."

"He was just being an *arsch*. Nothing to be worried about."

"Hans, you need to be careful. Don't get on the bad side of the Gestapo. They could make your life miserable."

I nodded, not wanting to spend any more time talking about that self-inflated *trottel*.

A waiter approached our table.

"One Weiss *bier*." I looked at both the girls. "Anna, Heidi, are you ready for another?"

"*Nein*," Anna said.

Heidi, in the middle of a swallow, shook her head.

"Well, how was everyone's day?" Dumb question. Most people answered fine or good, even if their day was lousy. I should have asked something else. Why was I still so nervous around Anna?

Heidi coughed and lightly tapped her chest. "An ordinary day at the Augsburg newspaper. The Americans and the English can be so blah. The Americans always talk about sports. The English are usually boring. Except now they're all in a buzz about Edward VIII abdicating the throne last month. And for a woman, no less." She flipped the back of her hand.

That remark made Anna laugh.

"Enough about tedious, mundane trappings." Heidi blotted her lips with a napkin. "Tell us what your day was like in the exciting aircraft industry."

The waiter brought my *bier*, and I took a large drink. "My work is just as boring as yours. You really don't want to know." Besides, she'd have no idea what I was talking about.

Anna slightly tilted her head and grinned, accentuating her ruby lips. "Hans, Heidi wants to know what you do at work. What better compliment? Tell her."

I took another drink. Now the glass was half-empty. "Not now. Maybe later."

"Fair enough," Anna said. "Let's not talk about work." She raised her glass, and we all toasted.

The rest of the evening, the three of us talked about our personal backgrounds.

Heidi shared she was the only child of two school-teachers from the small town of Berchtesgaden in Bavaria. She took a sip of wine, daintily holding the thin-stemmed glass with her thumb and index finger. "My childhood was a great one. My parents were loving. The only problem for me living in the mountains was being a klutz. I never learned to ski. My dad tried to teach me, but he said I had my mother's coordination. The truth is, I think I had his genes when it came to sports. He's just as clumsy as I am." She caught the attention of our waiter. "Another red wine, please."

I ordered another *bier*. "Anna, tell me more about your family." I crossed my legs and got more comfortable in my chair.

Anna's eyes sparkled. "I grew up in Garmisch, Bavaria, with two sisters and one brother. My parents owned a restaurant, and we all had duties. My brother and sisters were competitive skiers. I was the youngest and, of course, picked on the most. Although being the youngest was a pain in the *arsch*, it made me stronger. Strong enough to mold me into an Olympic downhill skier."

Heidi gasped. "That's so impressive. What I would give to have only a portion of your athletic ability." She leaned over the table. "And you, Hans, tell us about your life."

Talking about myself made me feel awkward. "I'm from Hamburg. My father is an auto mechanic. I attended Braunschweig Institute of Technology and graduated with a degree in mechanical engineering." I didn't elaborate on that, but I did tell them about my Olympic boxing experience.

The night moved on. We ate sautéed German sausage with bacon and apple sauerkraut, wiener schnitzel with lingonberry preserves, and one of my favorites, bratwurst and mustardy fried potatoes and braised cabbage. Eating large portions came natural to me, but these two ladies held their own.

Around 10:00, Heidi excused herself to the lavatory.

I took advantage of the few moments alone with Anna, leaning over and giving her a passionate kiss.

She put a hand behind my neck and held the kiss a long time.

"I don't want this night to end." My words soft, I was asking more than making a statement.

She kissed me again, moving her hand to my cheek. "This is not a good time."

Before I could ask why, Heidi came back and dropped her purse on the table. "Has the waiter brought our ticket?"

I shook my head. "*Nein*. But the night's on me, and my pleasure to do so."

Anna gave me a look that melted the soles of my shoes. "I'll make it up to you, I promise."

Heidi chuckled as though she'd had one too many drinks. "I wonder what she means by that, Hans." She rolled her eyes.

I placed my hand on Anna's. "Can you drive safely back to your apartment?"

She nodded and intertwined our fingers. "Yes, but thanks for asking." For a moment, it seemed as if she might be reconsidering extending the night. But then she stood and grabbed her coat off the back of the chair.

After escorting the ladies to Anna's car, I walked back into the hotel and headed to the elevator. It was too soon to let her know my feelings, but if our relationship continued, I knew I wanted to be with this woman long term. Was that something she might want too? Sometimes, I thought so. Other times, I had my doubts.

I stepped into the elevator and pressed the button to my floor unable to get my mind off Anna. Her mellow voice and the way she'd looked tonight sent a firestorm through my body. I wished I'd pushed the issue about going back to her apartment.

Getting off on the third floor, I walked down the hallway to my room and unlocked the door.

And stopped.

Something was different. Off. A strange odor accosted me. An odor that smelled like Hoermann.

I flipped on the light switch. What I saw made my heart rate double. The drawer on the bedside table was open—just a crack—but I knew I hadn't left it that way. Open drawers and cabinets drove me crazy. No, I'd carefully shut that drawer this morning before I'd left. Right after I'd put my journal inside.

CHAPTER 20

der 9. Fubruar 1937
Augsburg, Germany

I AM SURE SOMEONE BROKE INTO MY ROOM TWO WEEKS AGO.
I am not sure why. Getting in touch with Hoermann has
been impossible as he has been out of town. Although I
made a commitment, I am still torn between working for
the government autocrats I despise and helping the coun-
try I love. I keep wondering if I am sacrificing my values
and for what...

I accidentally knocked my small keepsake box to the
floor. When I picked up the items, my Olympic boxing
lapel pin was missing. I checked under the dresser and
the bedside table. Not there. Where was it? Losing that
pin would be a major disappointment. It was one of the
few things I had to remind me of that period in my life.
Since it was almost time to leave for work, I gave up
looking for now and finished dressing.

I opened my door and walking toward me was the
crooked-toothed Gestapo agent I'd had a run-in with at
the hotel bar.

He stepped in front of me.

I tried to squeeze by him.

He closed the gap. "Agent Schiffter wants to talk with you."

My mouth went dry, anticipating the verbal confrontation with a guy whose personality matched that of a dead animal. "I'm on my way to work."

"We've contacted Messerschmitt. He knows you won't be in today."

I scratched my temple. "What's this all about?" I kept my voice calm, not wanting to irritate Schiffter's lackey.

He motioned for me to follow him to the elevator, and I had no choice but to comply. When he pushed the button for the second floor, the cables groaned, the motor straining to lower the heavy metal box. A jolt rocked us, pushing me against the side of the elevator.

I glanced at the ceiling. "The hotel maintenance needs to check the gear box on the motor. Don't you think?"

The Gestapo errand-runner didn't even move. He could've been a statue.

The door opened, and we stepped onto the carpeted hallway, the muffled sound of our shoes in perfect step as we marched to the Gestapo office.

The lackey opened the door for me.

I stepped inside and focused on the last desk at the back of the room. Nothing had changed.

Schiffter rested his forearms on the desk and clasped his hands in front of him. His dark eyes bored a hole into my skull. His smirk told me I was in for a long day, for whatever trumped-up reason. The closer I got to his desk, the more he beamed a fake, painted-on smile. He didn't say a word, just pointed at the empty chair in front of his desk.

I pulled it out and sat, my shoulders rigid, my back tightening, bracing for what was about to happen. "What now?"

Anna had warned me about pissing off these people, but it was difficult pretending to kowtow to these thugs.

"You told us you had nothing to do with Heinrich Adler's death. Is that still your position?" Schiffter picked up a pencil and tapped it on the desk. The thud of the eraser echoed on the metal surface.

"Yes." I dropped my chin and glared at the pompous *arsch*, my chest heavy, my body sluggish.

He stopped tapping, opened the middle drawer of his desk, and picked something up.

I couldn't see the object gripped tight in his fist.

"Could this belong to you, *Herr* Pepperman?"

When he opened his fingers, my stomach bottomed out. The Olympic boxing pin. My mouth dropped open. I tried to speak but couldn't. My tongue seized up.

"I said, does this belong to you?" Schiffter's loud voice was shrouded in contempt.

Words finally formed. "Where did you get that?"

Scowling, he flicked the pen with his middle finger, spinning it like a top. "On the bank of the Lech River near where Adler's body was found. Is... this... yours?"

Someone was framing me. Who would do that? "I've never been on the Lech River where Adler died."

"I didn't ask if you'd been on the Lech River. I asked if this was your pin." He pointed at me. "And I said murdered. Adler was murdered."

"All right. Murdered. I didn't murder him." And I didn't claim the pin.

Schiffter's smug expression taunted me. "If you confess, *Herr* Pepperman, I can't make this go away, but I can make it easier for you. If you choose not to confess... well, then I can make your life miserable." His threatening words were piercing.

My brain began to shut down as though stuck in a quagmire. "I have nothing to add to what I've already told you."

Schiffter's face soured and bulged bright red. He leaned forward, wagging a yellowish, nicotine-stained finger at my chest. "You killed Adler, and you'll get the death penalty for it. I'll see to..." Eyes widening, he looked over my shoulder.

I turned and saw Hoermann walking toward us.

Schiffter's forehead grew slick with sweat. I couldn't tell if his reaction was one of intense fear or odd respect. But one thing was certain, Hoermann's presence changed the dynamic of the room.

He stopped at the edge of Schiffter's desk. "What's going on?" Although his voice came across soft, his tone was packed with authority.

Schiffter swiveled his chair to face Hoermann, rocking back and forth, the chair squeaking with each movement. "I'm arresting Hans Pepperman for the murder of Heinrich Adler." His voice lost its edge.

Hoermann picked up a brass paperweight, then set it back down. "What evidence do you have to substantiate your claim?"

Schiffter picked up the Olympic pin. "This is all the evidence I need."

Hoermann gave a lazy nod, as though he was thinking about his next words. "Did Pepperman say that was his pin?"

"*Nein*, but —"

Hoermann slapped the desk with an open hand. His face twisted with anger. "Did anyone see Pepperman the night of the murder where Adler was found?"

The room became graveyard silent as though the building were empty.

Schiffter offered Hoermann a blank-eyed stare.

"So," Hoermann continued, "you have no witness. But you do have an Olympic boxing pin that could belong to someone else. You mindless twit." He leaned in. "Pepperman is working for the Abwehr Military Intelligence Service under my direct command. You want to talk to him again, use protocol and ask me first. Is that clear?"

"And if I don't?" Schiffter stood, and there was a slight tremble in his hand.

"Then Wilhelm Canaris, the head of military intelligence, will haul your nutsack to Berlin." Hoermann removed papers from his jacket pocket and dropped them on Schiffter's desk.

He picked up the orders and started to read.

Hoermann snapped the papers back before Mr. Gestapo got through the first page. "Any questions?"

Schiffter's hardened, glassy-eyed stare said it all.

Hoermann stood, angrily pulling his pants up over his large stomach and left.

I quickly pushed back my chair and got up. A slingshot couldn't get me out of that office fast enough. I caught up with Hoermann in the elevator and pressed the lobby button.

As soon as the door closed, he grabbed my arm. "How in the hell did your boxing pin get there?"

I grabbed his hand, rolling his tight-gripped fingers off my bicep. "I was about to ask you that same question."

The elevator door opened, and Hoermann stepped out. "Let's carry this conversation to the car."

We left the Bauer, rounded the side of the building to his Mercedes, and got in.

"Hoermann, what the heck…?"

He stopped me and shook his fist at my nose. "Did you kill Heinrich Adler?"

Come on. Not him too. "Of course not. We had a barroom brawl that didn't end well for him. What's my motive for killing a guy I barely knew?"

"Then how did your Olympic pin end up in the hands of the Gestapo?"

"You tell me. I've been set up. At first I thought it was you but that—"

"Doesn't make sense." He grunted. "I just got you out of there."

"I know that now." But what I didn't know was how that smell, the same smell coming off Hoermann in this car, got in my hotel room.

Why would someone want me to take the fall for Adler's death?

CHAPTER 21

der 26. Fubruar 1937
Augsburg, Germany

I MAY HAVE OVERREACTED THINKING HOERMANN EXPECTED TOO much from me. I have talked with him weekly with no information to offer about suspicious activities. He reminds me to stay vigilant with my efforts but does not push me to dig deeper. I am actually beginning to like this guy...

Halfway through my pork sandwich, I noticed Ernst Fischer enter the lunchroom and waved him over to my table. Praying he didn't bring that rotten-smelling Limburger cheese that could make a corpse sit up, I offered him a seat. "I haven't seen much of you lately."

He pulled out a chair and sat down hard, both arms dropping limp at his sides. "Messerschmitt's been working me overtime."

I couldn't help but grin at the balding red-haired engineer. All five hairs on the top of his head stood straight up, reminding me of a North American porcupine. "What's the problem, my friend?"

He lifted the grease-stained paper bag holding his lunch and plopped it onto the table. "It's the fuselage on the medium range bomber. We can't seem to get all the requirements the Luftwaffe is looking for. Luftwaffe command wants a bomb load that's too heavy for the two-engine plane, and they don't want a long range four-engine aircraft. Which reminds me, can you educate me on the BF-109 power plant? We know the British bombers have Rolls Royce fighter plane engines. Maybe that's what Germany should use — prototype fighter plane engines on the medium range bomber." Ernst emptied his paper sack.

"What's in your lunch bowl?" Please say something that won't make me gag.

He opened the container, unleashing the most horrendous smell. The meat looked like raw chicken with strips of rubbery pineapple. Wilted lettuce made a fruit salad combination that resembled the remains of a bad hangover.

I could almost see the fumes wafting from the bowl. I subtly pinched my nostrils to block the pungent odor. "We'll talk about the 109 engine later."

"Sure, we'll talk later. What are your plans for the weekend?" He jabbed the meat and fruit combination with his fork and put it into his mouth. A piece of fruit fell on the table.

I swear it looked ready to crawl away to freedom.

I let go of my nose and leaned back in my chair to give my olfactory glands a break. "I'm seeing Anna tomorrow night." The weekend couldn't get here fast enough.

As he chewed, a piece of brownish-red lettuce slipped from his mouth. "Heidi and I are taking her parents out to dinner tonight."

If his table manners didn't improve, I shuddered to think of the impression he might make. "Ah, *gut* for you. This thing with Heidi, is it getting serious?"

He swallowed, then belched. Another food particle clung to the corner of his lip. "*Nein.*"

"Are you sure?"

"I do enjoy her company."

I liked Ernst, but I couldn't see them as a couple. "She is quite beautiful."

He repacked his mouth, chewed, then swallowed. "Agreed, but…" There was a long hesitation. "She wants to tell me every detail about her job, every interpretation about what the English and the Americans write in their newspapers. She's too informative." He made a crossing motion with his hands. "I don't like that in a person."

He didn't like a detailed person. Interesting. "But Ernst, your job demands detail."

He dropped his fork inside the bowl with a dumbfounded expression, head slightly tilted. "But my job's important."

Oh, he'd better be careful. "You best not tell Heidi that."

He cracked a smile. "I'm working on a PhD in aeronautical engineering. Do you think I'm that stupid?"

"I hope not. I surely hope not." I laughed so loud it drew the attention of the others in the lunchroom. An odd character Ernst. But the more I was around him, the more he became a good friend. People talked about him in a good way. He was smart and a more than capable engineer. The man's future was bright. Now if I could just get him to change his eating habits.

Friday night turned out to be atypical. I'd stayed at my office to go over data of grades of oil used in the journal bearing in the BF-109 engine. I glanced at my watch at 11:02 p.m. Exhausted, I laid my head down on my desk and dozed off.

Click. Click. Click.

I sat up quickly and looked around. What was that noise? Had someone turned the handle on my door?

Click. Click. Click. The sound came again.

A sting zipped through my chest. "Who's there?" My skin prickled. My arm hair spiked. "Who's there?"

No answer.

I picked up a letter opener—the only thing I had in my office even close to a weapon. I flipped the lock and slowly opened the door.

A spooky *creak* echoed down the long hallway.

I stuck my head around the door frame.

It was dark except for the sliver of light reflecting off the walls through the windows from the lights outside.

I looked both ways. My throat closed up. I swallowed hard and moved cautiously toward the exit door. The *klomp, klomp, klomp* of my leather-soled shoes on the concrete added to my edginess, but I was ready to defend myself.

Whack.

Something hit my head. Suddenly the floor was spinning.

"Hans, can you hear me? Are you okay?" A blurred Ernst knelt over me, his voice sounding as though it was underwater.

My head throbbed like a second heartbeat, and I gingerly touched where it hurt the most. Ow. I jerked my hand away. Blood covered my fingers.

Ernst handed me a white handkerchief.

I pressed it carefully to the wound and tried to stand.

Ernst pushed me back down. "Maybe you should sit awhile. Did you see who did this?"

"*Nein*. Someone must have come up behind me." The cobwebs were shaking loose, and my eyes began to focus. That's when I noticed Ernst had a knot over his left eye and his forehead was bleeding. "What happened to you?"

"I had my keys out when someone crashed through the door, knocking me to the ground. I couldn't see who it was. Then I saw you on the floor."

"Why are you even here?" I removed the handkerchief. The bleeding seemed to have slowed.

"Heidi's dad became ill at the restaurant, and she took him back to their hotel. I needed the blueprint of the medium range bomber to take back to my apartment."

I stared at Ernst with a stern look. "You know we're not to take work home."

"I do it all the time. What management does not know will not hurt them. Besides, some of my best work has been after a pitcher of *bier*. Do I need to get you to a doctor?"

"Head wounds like this aren't as bad as they look. What about you? Do you want to see someone about your face?" I got to my feet.

"I'm fine."

I grabbed his shoulder. "Wait. Did you come through the gate? And did the guard see you?"

"Of course."

"If you came through the gate, how did the person who attacked me get inside the facility?"

Ernst slowly patted the egg-sized knot over his eye. "Security keeps a log of who comes in and the time they enter."

"Exactly," I said. "There's no record of who leaves, but we all have to go past the security guard to get out. Right?"

Ernst nodded. "We should tell the guard what happened."

"*Nein. Nein.*" Ernst couldn't find out I was working with Hoermann and the military intelligence. "Don't say anything. Not until we know the guard isn't part of a security breach. I'll tell Messerschmitt Monday." I was up to my neck in this now. *Verdammt.*

CHAPTER 22

der 27. Fubruar 1937
Augsburg, Germany

My head is sore from the attack last night, but I did not get stitches. The wound should heal quickly on its own. I will call Hoermann Monday morning about the incident. Right now, I am looking forward to my date with Anna...

Another snowstorm had moved into the area. From my hotel room, I could barely see the buildings across the street. I closed the curtains and eased onto the bed.

The Augsburg bell tower clock struck ten. My head still ached from the assault. Just as I'd thought the spy operation was no big deal, last night happened. Now I had reservations again. But it was too late to back out.

Should I carry a weapon? A lot of good that would do when I couldn't hit an advertising poster ten feet in front of me. I suppose with practice I could learn to shoot. Did I want to? I was an engineer, not a marksman.

I gently touched my head wound. I had to tell Anna. She'd see it anyway. Maybe I should call her. She might want to cancel because of the storm. I pushed off the bed, dressed, and went downstairs to use the phone.

The lobby was fairly empty. So was the bar. I blamed the storm for the lack of people as I walked across the marble floor. The empty silence made the usually crowded space feel cavernous. I waved to Elsa, the registration clerk. "How's Dieter?"

Making two fists in front of her chest, she jabbed twice.

I gave her a thumbs up. A few weeks ago I'd taught her four-year-old son to take a fighter's stance. Cute kid.

Someone was in the phone booth, so I had to wait.

Outside the front windows, huge flakes drifted aimlessly to the ground and disappeared among the other ice crystals. The falling snow was so peaceful it seemed to cleanse the world of all its dirtiness. An illusion, I was sure. War clouds appeared to be gathering over Europe once again. I prayed that catastrophe wouldn't happen.

The person in the phone booth finally left.

Taking his place, I pulled some coins out of my pocket, closed the door, and dialed Anna.

"Anna Beck, *guten morgen*." Her tone came across as chilly as the morning.

"*Guten morgen*. This is Hans."

"I was thinking about you." Her voice softened with joy. "This snow. Ah, it's so much. Why don't we… ?"

"I understand. It's too much to put up with. We can have dinner another night."

She laughed. "Hans, I was about to say why don't we stay in. I've already picked up veal and a bottle of Schnapps. How does that sound to you?"

While she couldn't see my happy grin reflecting off the phone booth glass, I could, and it made me smile bigger. "That sounds perfect. What time?"

"Hmm... six. Are you catching the train?"

"Yes."

"Don't worry about the last train back. You won't need it." Her sultry voice excited me.

Heat sizzled down my body making me completely forget my headache. I still picked up ice from the bar. Back in my room, I put it on the wound. The incident last night made me realize espionage life wasn't for the faint of heart. I had two choices — stay true to my values and defend my country or take the coward's way out and quit. I was no coward. Besides, I was pissed someone knocked me out, and I relished the thought of getting even.

The snow continued all day, reaching a depth of ten to twelve inches. The train, if weather hadn't made it late, would leave the boarding area at 5:30.

I put on my overcoat, wrapped a scarf around my neck, and headed to the door. Before I turned the knob, I ran back to the bathroom to get my toothbrush.

The train was on time. The short ride to Fuggerei housing project gave little opportunity to think what I would tell Anna about the cut on my head. I didn't want to tell her what had happened at my office because it would draw suspicion from the Gestapo.

The train stopped, and I tucked the scarf tighter around my neck, shoving the ends deep into my coat. Snow blew in my face, and I lowered my head, barely able to read the numbers on her apartment door.

Knock. Knock. The cold door stung my bare knuckles.

Anna opened the door. Her tight red sweater left little mystery about what was underneath. Her sculptured cheekbones framed moist ruby lips. But her eyes, her eyes got me every time. They were easily the most seductive part of her beauty.

"Come in." Her soft tone almost buckled my knees.

I scraped my feet on the door mat and stepped inside.

She softly touched my cheek, then kissed the corner of my lips. "You look very handsome tonight."

Warmth flooded my chest. "*Danke.*"

"I'll take your coat and scarf." She hung them on the rack behind the door.

The room, lit with candles, smelled of vanilla. Soft music played on the phonograph.

The violins. Good grief. They were too squeaky. "This music, Anna. Who's the composer?"

"Arnold Schoenberg. His string quartet arrangement is so beautiful. Do you like it?"

I'd never heard of the guy. Or a string quartet. "I love string quartets."

She gave me a knowing smile that said *you're lying.* "Would you like a drink? Is Schnapps okay?"

"Schnapps is fine. Do you like that particular liqueur?"

She dropped her chin. "It puts me in a certain mood."

And that was a mood I loved. "Pour yourself a double." I grinned.

A red cloth covered the dining table. On top of it a candle floated in a bowl of water.

"I hope you like veal za'atar flatbread. It won't take long to warm in the oven."

I nodded. "Let's have a drink before we eat." One drink usually jumpstarted my appetite.

"One drink coming up." Anna turned her back to me and headed to the kitchen. She looked just as good from behind as she did from the front. Her strong shoulders, small waist, and deliciously curved hips projected the image of an athlete.

I sat in the middle of the sofa, my arms resting on top of the back cushion.

She returned to the living room with a drink in each hand and stopped in front of me. Straddling both of my legs, she sat inches from my face, her eyes focused on mine.

The stare sent a clear message. The night was going to be exciting. "Maybe we should skip dinner?"

Chuckling, she handed me a glass of Schnapps and rolled off my legs to sit next to me. "You're a very interesting man, Hans."

Interesting good or interesting bad? Maybe I shouldn't have suggested we put off dinner. I squared my body, facing her. "What makes you say that?" I took a sip of my drink and swallowed hard as it burned down my throat. She hadn't been light on the liquor.

"You're handsome, big, and smart. Every woman's dream." She took a sip from her glass. "Adding to the mystique, I know very little about you."

She was the mystery. I was a former boxer and a dull engineer. "I can solve that problem, but I need to see you more often."

"Oh, by all means, it would be my pleasure."

We toasted.

"Anna, time spent with you is the best part of my day." I thought true love was a lie, but I was beginning to change my mind.

She set her drink down on the end table and cupped her hands over my ears.

I grimaced and pulled back.

"Is something wrong?" She sounded hurt.

I chuckled. "*Nein*, but I must tell you a stupid thing that happened."

She leaned back, resting against the sofa arm. "Tell me."

"Well…" I touched the top of my head. "I slipped getting out of the shower and hit my head on the sink."

Anna's eyes widened, and she touched her mouth. "Oh, my, did you need stitches?"

"Probably, but head wounds bleed a lot, and it looks worse than it really is. I just wanted to let you know the gash is still very tender."

A slight grin appeared through her parted fingers. "I'll be careful. I promise." She glanced toward the kitchen. "The flatbread should be ready. Let's go to the table."

I helped her off the couch. The food smelled wonderful, and the drink had sharpened my appetite.

Anna pulled down the oven door, removed the round meat pie with two potholders, and set it on the counter, cutting it into wedges. "Would you bring the plates from the table?"

I carried the white porcelain plates trimmed in green to the kitchen.

"One or two slices?" she asked.

"Three."

The corners of her mouth peaked upward. "Three it is."

She took two slices.

I pulled a chair out for her and laid a white linen napkin on her lap, then took my place across from her at the small rectangular table.

The string quartet music set the stage for the evening, and the stout drink did its part. We were obviously hungry because the conversation stopped.

Halfway through dinner, I grinned at the glob of red sauce clinging to her lip.

She looked at me. "What?"

I tapped the corner of my lip with my index finger.

Anna dabbed the tomato sauce with her napkin and gave me a half-smile of embarrassment.

"Do you want to know what I like about you?" I asked.

Chewing, she nodded.

"I love the way your eyes smile."

She swallowed and leaned back in her chair. "That's one of the most beautiful things anyone has ever said to me."

"It's true. I love every minute I'm with you."

The night got better the longer we talked, drank, and laughed. I was falling for this woman, and I hoped the feeling was mutual.

About midnight Anna grabbed my hand and led me to the bedroom.

Except for the thin veil of light coming through the curtains, I sat in complete darkness at the foot of the bed.

She went to the window and pulled the curtains back.

The storm had moved. A full moon shone through the gnarled branches of a leafless tree.

She spun slowly in my direction.

All I could see was a perfect silhouette. But I felt her gaze on me as she kicked off her shoes, crossed her arms, and pulled the sweater over her head.

Her trousers fell to the floor next as she padded toward me.

She took my breath. And the breath after that. And the one after that.

CHAPTER 23

der 1. März 1937
Augsburg, Germany

SATURDAY NIGHT WITH ANNA TOOK MY MIND OFF THE ATTACK
at my office. My head is not as sore today but aches enough
to remind me not to run a comb through my hair. I called
Hoermann early this morning. After work, he is taking me to
a location out of my element and into his. He chose the Boar's
Head Club, north of the downtown area...

Hoermann had asked that I meet him five blocks up
Volkhartstr at 8:00 p.m. The streets were mostly empty.
The night air hung heavy, reaching deep into my core
with its numbing cold. I didn't know if I was ready to face
the dangers associated with Hoermann and his spies. But
I must step up for my country, be willing to take the risk.

At least, I didn't have to wait for him. He was right
on time, and I quickly opened the car door and slid in —
to a pleasant surprise. The disagreeable smell of body
odor had been replaced with the agreeable musk scent
of cologne. Wondering why the change, I wanted to ask.
But what could I say that wouldn't be offensive?

I Ioermann looked both ways before driving through
the intersection.

I tapped him on the upper arm. "I'm not familiar with the Boar's Head Club."

With one hand resting on the top of the steering wheel, he gave a sheepish grin that forced a crease in his fleshy cheeks. "It's a comedy club. A burlesque show. I've been there a couple of times. There shouldn't be too many people on a Monday night. We can talk and not be disturbed."

The clandestine thing with spies? I could never get used to that type of work.

He drove by a sleazy, dark gray stone building where flashing red neon lights spelled out *Boar's Head Club*. He parked the car on a side street, and we got out and walked a short distance to a heavy steel door. One big floodlight glowed brightly overhead.

I must have looked hesitant because he said, "This club is a throwback to the speakeasy establishments during prohibition time in America." He knocked three times, then turned to me and shrugged. "Part of the ambiance to make it appear real."

Someone opened a peep hole, shut it, and opened the door. "Ah, *Herr* Hoermann, how good to see you. Come in."

For him to have been to this place only a couple of times, he must've made a big impression.

Shutting the door behind us, the man asked, "Your usual table, *Herr* Hoermann?"

They knew his favorite table. He'd been feeding me a line of horse *scheisse*.

The room was maybe a quarter filled with patrons, mostly men. A row of empty stools covered in black leather ran along the long marble-topped bar. Dusty, half-empty liquor bottles lined shelves in front of a mirror. How long had it been since the supply had been restocked? Obviously, cleaning was not a priority.

Up on stage, a man and a woman told lewd jokes to an audience that wasn't listening. The girl, scantily dressed, wore heavy makeup, dramatic false eyelashes, and a huge red wig. The man wore a brown pinstriped suit with a watch fob that hung to his knees.

Some ladies came from a side entrance next to the stage and cuddled up to the men in the audience.

Minutes later, the men and women got up from the tables in couples and walked back through the same door.

This was a brothel pretending to be a nightclub. "Hoermann, you devil," I whispered.

But mesmerized by the long-legged woman on stage, he didn't hear me.

His attention strayed only when a generously hipped waitress asked, "Would you gentlemen like to order?"

"Yes, yes, of course." He reached into his coat pocket and pulled out a tobacco pouch, unzipped it, and filled his pipe. He huffed several times on the pipe until it was lit and exhaled a large, gray billow of smoke

I smelled the same cherry aroma as before. I tapped his large arm. "That tobacco has a unique smell. Tell me about it."

He removed the pipe from his mouth. "A cherry blend. My pipe is a Yello Bole I picked up on a trip to New York City and is a popular brand in America."

"I've only seen you smoke a pipe a few times." I was beginning to really like this man.

"It's a bad habit, but I enjoy a good smoke from time to time." He sucked in a large breath with his pipe in his mouth. Red embers burned in the pipe bowl. He exhaled a billow of smoke twice as big as the first. "Hans, what would you like?" His attention returned to the woman on the stage.

"Weisse *bier*." I smiled at the rotund intelligence officer's infatuation with the long-legged performer.

The waitress shifted her weight, waiting on Hoermann to decide.

"Hmm… a weisse *bier* for me too."

She turned and walked back to the bar.

He loosened his tie and unbuttoned the stressed collar. "Hans, when you called me, I noticed urgency in your voice about this meeting. What's going on?"

The waitress brought our *biers*.

Hoermann took a large drink before setting the mug down.

"Last Friday I worked late at the aircraft factory. Around 11:00 p.m., someone tried to enter my office. I went to see who was there. When I stepped into the hallway, I was hit over the head and knocked out."

He snapped to attention. "Did you see who it was?"

"*Nein*. Ernst Fischer, one of the engineers at the plant, found me on the floor."

"Ernst Fischer?" He lowered his gaze and raised his voice. "Why was he at the factory at that time of night?"

The way he said Fischer's name made me think he knew him. "It's a long story, but he was hurt by the same person who knocked me out. He didn't get a look at the individual either."

"Have you told anyone what happened?" He took another drink, finishing off his *bier*.

"I was going to tell Messerschmitt this morning, but he was out of the office today."

Hoermann leaned over the table. "Don't mention this to anyone. I will talk with Messerschmitt tomorrow. What about Fischer? He must keep this quiet also." His voice was barely audible.

"I told him not to say anything."

Hoermann had a far-off look in his eyes as he tapped the ends of his fingers together.

He knew something. Something he had no intention of telling me.

CHAPTER 24

der 18. März 1937
Augsburg, Germany

A COUPLE OF WEEKS HAVE PASSED SINCE THE MEETING WITH Hoermann at the Boar's Head Club. Messerschmitt is aware of the attack on Fischer and me. Pressure is being placed on Messerschmitt and Germany's armament production. Twelve-hour days are not uncommon at the factory. Something is going on politically, and many people at work feel war is inevitable. I hope they are wrong. Messerschmitt has called a special meeting this morning. I better get going…

By 7:30 a.m., the hallway leading to the cafeteria was already jammed with employees.

"Hans, wait up." Ernst muscled his way through the workers. "What's this meeting about?" he asked, half out of breath.

"Your guess is as good as mine." I was lucky to find two empty chairs for us midway to the podium. In meetings like this, everyone wanted to sit at the back of the room.

Messerschmitt, accompanied by Hoermann, entered from a side door.

The noisy room quieted almost immediately, the silence a symbol of the respect Messerschmitt had from the factory workers.

Fischer nudged me with his elbow. "Who's that fat fellow with the Hitler mustache?" His words were muffled.

I shrugged. Hoermann had stressed that I couldn't let anyone find out I was an undercover agent with the military intelligence—even though he'd seemed to recognize Fischer's name when I'd mentioned it at the Boar's Head Club. Fischer didn't seem to know Hoermann, but did Hoermann know of Fischer? And why?

Messerschmitt adjusted the height of the microphone stand and tapped the mic to see if it was turned on. "Good morning." He turned his head and cigarette coughed. "I want to introduce Otto Hoermann of the Abwehr Military Intelligence Service. His message is important. Please pay attention." He sat, crossed his legs, and turned sideways in the chair, looking very uneasy.

Hoermann stood, buttoned his belly-strained coat, and stepped to the microphone. "*Danke, Herr* Messerschmitt. I want to thank each of you for your contributions to the Fatherland. Your work is top secret and other countries want our technology. Be alert. If you notice anything suspicious, inform your supervisor immediately." Hoermann's physical appearance might be lacking, but his baritone voice commanded respect, and all eyes in the room seemed focused on him.

Fischer leaned toward me. "You did tell Messerschmitt about what happened to us?"

I nodded. "He knows."

He leaned in again. "That happened weeks ago. Why is that Hoermann fellow just now telling us to be on the watch for suspicious things?"

I shrugged again.

Hoermann's speech was filled with propaganda about the greater Germany. His oratory skill didn't match *Der Fuhrer's* but was close. Even so, the talk lasted too long.

Fischer was the first to rise from his chair. "Are we still on with the ladies for tomorrow night?"

I stood. "The Ratskeller restaurant on Friday night is going to be crowded. I hope Anna made reservations."

Fischer cupped his hand over his mouth and yawned. "Why didn't you make the reservations?"

"I offered, but she was adamant." Anna's strong personality drew me to her.

Fischer yawned again as though he hadn't had enough sleep last night. "I bet she'll want the same table and asks for the same waiter."

What did that mean? And how would he know? Could Fischer and Anna have been more than friends at one time? I looked at him. I chuckled — not a chance.

CHAPTER 25

der 19. März 1937
Augsburg, Germany

THE MEETING YESTERDAY WITH MESSERSCHMITT AND HOERMANN at the aircraft factory left everyone a little paranoid. Little did they know just how on edge they should be. Fischer and I had paid the price for being at the right place at the wrong time. Our head wounds prove it.

Fischer will drive Anna and Heidi to the restaurant because they all live in the same Fuggerei housing project. I will meet them at 8:00 p.m. Anna dropped all sorts of hints that she had to leave Augsburg early tomorrow morning. No overnight for me...

I could walk from the Bauer Hotel to the Ratskeller, the distance only a few blocks. I pushed through the revolving door of the hotel lobby, a sharp blast of north wind stinging my face. Grasping the neck of my coat, I fastened the top button.

The breeze howled as it whipped around the corners of the building. Something different about the whistling sounds caught me off guard. The strong draft blew a clump of snow off the angled roof of a business, and it splattered on the ice-crystalled sidewalk. Streetlights highlighted my breath.

For no apparent reason, a cold chill gripped my body that made me feel as if I was being watched. I turned around, then looked across the street. No one.

I'd only walked half a block when two men exited from a nearby alley.

Their black fedoras were pulled down tight, the collars of their coats flush to their faces. One had a cigarette dangling from the corner of his lips. "Do you have a light?" The tobacco stick bounced up and down in his mouth with each word.

I shook my head, buying time to figure out which one was the biggest threat so I could take him out first.

The other inched closer. "So, what do you have? How about money? You got any money?"

I removed my hands from my coat pocket and raised them to the halt position. A gesture I hoped would indicate I didn't want trouble.

They stepped closer, the man directly in front of me in position for a power right cross.

I extended my fist. *Pow.* A perfectly placed punch to the idiot's nose.

He fell back, his body stiff as a department store mannequin.

The other joker looked at his friend lying on the ground, shocked.

I gave him a quick kick to the family jewels, and he went down into a fetal position, whimpering like a frightened rabbit.

I stepped around the moaning thug and headed to the restaurant. Flexing my right hand, I looked at my large knuckle. Hitting someone on a cold night, not a good idea, but I had no choice. I shook off the pain and kept walking.

What an odd encounter. The pair had been dressed too well for ordinary thieves. And if they weren't thieves, who were they, and what had they wanted? Was I a random target or part of some plan? All this spy stuff was getting to me.

When I got to the restaurant, Anna, Heidi, and Ernst were seated next to the maître d's podium. The smell of roasting pork from the kitchen piqued my appetite as I laughed to myself about the two pseudo-tough boys who'd tried to bully me tonight and ended up on the receiving end instead.

Fischer stood, tugging on his trousers, then buttoned his suit coat. "Why the big grin, Hans?"

I waved him off. "I'll tell you later."

Anna stepped forward and kissed my cheek.

I reciprocated, then reached one arm around Heidi's shoulder and gave her a hug.

Anna turned to the maître d.' "Reservations for Anna Beck."

A young man flipped through pages. "Yes. We have your table ready in the center of the dining room."

Anna put her palm down on the stand. "Excuse me. I did not request a table at that location."

The young man glanced down at the seating arrangement. "I'm sorry. There must be a mistake. Someone wrote down a table in the center of the room."

Anna inhaled and exhaled in obvious frustration. "I requested the table in the corner next to the fireplace and for my waiter to be Frederick."

The nervous young man adjusted his black bow tie and cleared his throat. "Let me check to see if the table by the fireplace is available." He quickly walked to the doorway entrance, looked inside, then returned a lot less enthusiastically. "I'm so sorry, *fräulein,* but the table you requested is occupied. To make it up to you, your meal will be on the Ratskeller." He looked at Anna through sheepish eyes.

She pointed to the room, her face tight, lips barely parted. "*Nein.* You go tell those people to move and have the Ratskeller pay for their dinner. I specifically asked for the table in the corner next to the fireplace, and I was told that it would be available at the time I requested."

The young man reminded me of a scolded dog as he walked — tail between his legs — into the dining area.

I watched as he approached the customers. Luckily, they nodded without much fuss and stood as a waiter moved their plates and drinks to the table mistakenly assigned to us. The free meal no doubt made the process easier.

The spring in his step as he came back was obvious. "*Fräulein,* your table will be ready in a moment. Please allow us to still pay for your dinner, and I deeply apologize for the inconvenience."

Anna smiled, a genuine smile. "We all make mistakes. But the issue is how we handle those mishaps. You did a marvelous job, and I will tell your employer this establishment is fortunate to have you."

The glow in the man's face told me everything about how the compliment made him feel.

I'd made mistakes in the past, and I too appreciated when people noticed my efforts to correct them.

After our table by the fireplace was cleaned, we took our seats.

Frederick, Anna's favorite waiter — the one she introduced to me our first time here — approached us with glasses of water. As he set the drinks in front of us, she asked, "How's your family?"

"Very well. Thank you for asking." His expression turned warm. Leaving the menus, he gave us a few minutes before he returned to take our orders.

Anna looked at Heidi. "So what did you translate for the Augsburg newspaper today?"

She adjusted the cuffs of her white silk blouse. "Well, America is obsessed with Germany's military advancements. A writer for the *New York Times* discussed the BF-109 fighter plane engine. What makes this engine so special, Hans?"

It seemed as though Heidi was always asking about my work. "It's powerful and fast." I shrugged.

Heidi interlocked her fingers and nodded. "Fast and powerful. I see." She tilted her head to the side as though she judged my answer as weak and superficial.

I leaned forward in my chair. "We've gone over this before. Even if I told you the mechanics of the engine, you wouldn't understand." I grinned, taking the edge off what could be interpreted as a curt response.

Heidi's scrunched nose reminded me of a little girl. She slouched back in her chair and smiled. "Hans, you are such a bore. I give you the best compliment I can by showing interest in you and your work. Come on, just tell me one thing about the German marvel."

I softly tapped the table. "It doesn't have a carburetor."

Heidi folded her arms across her chest, looked at Anna and Fischer, then back at me. "What's a carburetor?"

Everyone laughed at Heidi's typical dry humor.

After a good meal and a few drinks, it was time to close out the evening. Fischer was not only a good coworker but a great friend. I was getting to know Heidi better and felt comfortable teasing her.

Wishing Anna didn't have to leave town in the morning, I gave her a light kiss goodbye outside the restaurant and watched her walk down the sidewalk.

As I headed back to the hotel alone, I couldn't help checking over my shoulder and wondering if I had been targeted earlier. And if so, why?

CHAPTER 26

der 22. März 1937
Augsburg, Germany

THE WEEKEND SEEMED SHORT. MY WORK ON THE 109'S ENGINE
probably helped pass the time. Fischer was taking work home
to get ahead. My goal too. If I get caught, it could lead to trou-
ble. But as he said, "What management does not know cannot
not hurt them." I remember Barron telling me about Russia
wanting our fighter plane technology and how important the
fuel injections system is to the plane's performance. In light
of that, sneaking the engine schematics out of the factory has
been a mistake. A mistake I hope I will not regret...

When I got to work, the guard at gate was checking
everyone's identification cards closely. He stopped me and
ordered that I report to Messerschmitt's office immediately.

My shoulders tensed. Did he already know I'd taken
work home?

Fischer met me in the hallway a few feet from the
cafeteria. "Hans, we have time for coffee. Come join me."
What was with his huge grin? He looked ridiculous.

Shifting my briefcase to my left hand while unbut-
toning my overcoat, I kept walking. "Messerschmitt
wants to see me."

Fischer gave me a thumbs up as I passed. "Maybe you're getting a pay raise."

"Not counting on it." Not if Messerschmitt had discovered how I'd spent my weekend. Then I'd be getting fired.

Messerschmitt's beautiful secretary greeted me with her usual sexy grin. "*Gut morgen, Herr* Pepperman. *Herr* Messerschmitt is waiting for you."

I loved her soft, baritone voice. In spite of what I might be walking into, the way she directed her grin at me was a boost to my ego. "*Danke.*" I smiled back, giving her a slight nod, and stepped into the office.

Messerschmitt stood at the window, his back to me—feet spread, one hand on his hip, a cigarette between his first two fingers. And he wasn't alone. There were two other men with him... one of them Hoermann.

The tension in my shoulders tripled. This summons was about more than me taking work home. The fact that Hoermann was here confirmed it. I glanced at him questioningly, but he avoided my gaze. Not good.

Messerschmitt walked from the window and took a seat at his desk. He crushed the cigarette so hard into the ashtray the tobacco splintered into different directions, his glare so intense, I looked away.

Had Messerschmitt found out about my ties to the military intelligence? Or had Hoermann let my boss in on our secret? Was he going to fire me? Or something worse? I felt queasy.

Settling onto the couch, Hoermann folded his arms across his chest, refusing to look at me in a way that negated every conversation we'd ever had.

No, he hadn't let Messerschmitt in on anything. Did Hoermann think I had?

"Have a seat." The other man in the room was the first to speak. Tall with a formidable physique, he had blond hair that still showed the tracks from the comb he'd obviously pushed through it earlier this morning. He pointed at the chair across from Messerschmitt's desk, the gesture a command not a request.

My mind reeling, I sat and dropped my briefcase next to the chair. I didn't want to give anything away until I knew what this was about. It could be nothing, right? Not even a little part of me believed that. It was definitely something. And probably something big.

The blond man moved the chair from the desk with little effort, squared it in front of me and sat, his posture a little too starched — just like his black uniform, brown shirt, and black tie. "I'm Dieter Keitel with the Reich Security Central Office of the Gestapo."

Gestapo. My breathing growing shallow, I risked another look at Hoermann — whose refusal to acknowledge me never wavered. There were two reasons the Gestapo would be here. They'd discovered my secret meetings with Hoermann. Or they still linked me to Heinrich Adler's death.

"Move your chair to face me," Keitel said. "I want to look at you." His bass voice demanded as much respect as his chiseled jawline and steel blue eyes.

My heart thrashed at the power coming off him, especially since he'd so completely directed it at me, but I did what he asked, trying not to show my anxiety. Until now,

I'd never feared another man. But this man? He not only expected that fear, he'd earned it.

Keitel leaned forward in his chair, his stare piercing.

I don't know what kicked up my heartbeat harder — wondering what he was going to say or waiting for him to say it.

"You. Are. A. Russian. Spy." Not even under the guise of a question, those five words came at me loud and clear.

And they weren't what I'd expected. At least, the part about Russia. *Spy. Spy. Spy.* The shock of his accusation boomed inside my head. What had put me on the Gestapo's radar? All Hoermann had asked me to do was watch for potential espionage. For him. For my country. Not for Russia. And I'd seen nothing to report.

"Eyes on me," Keitel instructed gruffly.

I did as he told me. I was innocent. So why was my heart taking off in a deep sprint? And Russia? Was this guy crazy? Brushing my hand against my chest, I kept my gaze from straying toward Hoermann and looked at Messerschmitt instead, even though getting fired had suddenly become the least of my concerns.

"I repeat," Keitel said, "you are a Russian spy."

I gripped the chair. "*Nein*, I'm not a spy." My words were battle ready. I knew what the Gestapo did to spies. And I didn't like having my character questioned. "I love my country. I can't even speak Russian." As if any of that mattered, but my desperation didn't know that.

"Hoermann." Keitel motioned for him to come closer.

Why hadn't Hoermann mentioned I was on the same side? Why didn't he now? He could've changed the way this conversation was going with a few easy words.

Picking up a suitcase I hadn't noticed before, Hoermann set it on Messerschmitt's desk, still acting as if I didn't exist. His cold demeanor made me sweat.

For a few moments, the room was bizarrely silent except for the clock on the wall as it ticked to the cadence of my racing heart.

The Gestapo agent *tapped, tapped, tapped* on the side of the black case. He flipped the gold latches, and they popped against the leather case. He lifted the top. "Do you know what this is, Hans?"

Inside was a box with five or six knobs and dials with what looked like a transmitter button and a headset.

I shrugged, but my shoulders felt stiff. "A communication radio?"

The agent nodded. "A shortwave radio to be exact. Do you know where we found it?"

"How would I know that?" I shook my head. "I've never seen it before."

"Interesting… since it was under your bed at the Bauer Hotel." Each word he spoke was slow, distinct, and dipped in accusation.

Those *arschlochs* had been in my room. Someone was framing me. "That's not mine." I swallowed hard, but my mouth was so dry it was difficult to speak.

The Gestapo agent stood. "Do you know how Germany deals with spies? With traitors? With *müll*?"

Der Tod. The Death. "I don't know how the radio got there." I swiped my palms on my pants. "I'm not a spy. You're making a mistake." This time I couldn't help looking at Hoermann.

He sat motionless, cold, detached. He may as well have been a statue in a park. Why wasn't he defending me? Or at least saying something?

Keitel hiked me off the chair by my collar. "Put your hands behind your back." He reached inside his coat pocket and pulled out a pair of Clejuso handcuffs and locked them around my wrists so tight they pinched my skin and cut off the circulation.

I looked at Hoermann, past his soiled tie and bulging girth, and he looked at the floor. I'd agreed to help him, and he'd sold me out. "Pathetic slob," I whispered under my breath.

Meanwhile, Messerschmitt turned away and lit another cigarette. He wasn't any better. He knew how hard I'd worked to correct the problem with the 109, how hard I'd worked here for him, yet he offered no support either.

I had no friends in this room. And that amped my fear into anger. I'd been painted into a corner with no way out. Clearly Hoermann and Messerschmitt weren't going to be any help. That I felt betrayed was an understatement. I clinched my jaw, my chest heavy, scrambling for a way to prove my innocence.

Agent Keitel grabbed my arm and pulled me toward the door. "Let's go."

I jerked from his grip. "Where are you taking me?" I'd heard stories, whispers about Gestapo tactics, that melted my anger into fear once more.

Keitel latched onto my bicep, his hold stronger and forceful. "I said move. Don't make this difficult."

"Hans, just come with us." Hoermann finally decided to speak.

I didn't like what he said. Why should I listen when he'd done nothing to help me? "I trusted you." Each word was an accusation.

Picking up on the fact that I was about to spill everything we'd talked privately about in the past, he grabbed my other arm, his stare warning me to say nothing else. "If you're not guilty of espionage, you'll be released. Now move."

"You and I both know exactly what I'm not guilty of," I mumbled as he walked me to the door. I didn't bother looking back to Messerschmitt. No better than Hoermann, my boss could go to hell. I hoped he choked on that filthy tobacco stick.

Walking down the hallway in handcuffs was humiliating. About thirty people stood by their office doors gawking at me. Some of the looks were of disgust, others appeared sympathetic.

I passed Fischer leaning against his doorframe. His eyes were fixed on me, but I had no idea what he was thinking. I'd expected at least a little something from him. A smile of encouragement. A glance of empathy. We were friends, weren't we?

Hoermann opened the back door to Keitel's car, helped me in, and slid in next to me—a little too close.

Keitel drove us out of the factory parking lot.

The silence was interrupted only by the shifting of gears and the thud of tires passing over potholes in the road.

The longer we drove, the more regret gnawed at my gut. I should never have agreed to help Hoermann. "Damn it, someone talk to me. Where are you taking me?"

"Away from Augsburg," Hoermann answered with disgust, as if I'd been the betrayer.

There was still time to become that. "I'm not guilty of anything."

"Then you won't mind telling us all about the short-wave radio and who you are working with."

I wanted to say, *I'm working with you.* But something made me bite back the words. I kicked the back of the seat instead.

Keitel swerved off the road, hitting the brakes so hard my head bounced against the window. Turning, he pointed at me. "You kick the back of this seat again, and I'll pull you out of the car. Believe me, you won't like what happens next." The rage in his words made me a believer.

I sat back, thinking about torture — pulling finger-nails, beatings, cutting off ears — then death. Not a good picture. Did things like that actually happen, or were they stories spread to keep German citizens in line? The more I learned about the Nazi Party, the more I hated their ideology.

About forty-five minutes later, the car turned onto a dirt road that led to a rundown, old stone house that looked as though it should be deserted. It wasn't. A single empty vehicle sat parked in front.

Hoermann forced me out, and we followed Keitel up the concrete steps and through a heavy, weath-er-beaten door.

The stale, metallic smell of blood mixed with urine and vomit hung in the air, giving a new validity to those stories of torture. Were these smells the remnants of people who were here before me? Did their deaths linger on the walls and the floor?

Keitel dragged me to the middle of the room and forced me into a metal chair in front of a table. He stepped to the other side to sit in a matching chair that had been pushed close to a large floodlight.

Not terrible. A floodlight I could handle. I relaxed a little until I saw another table against the wall lined with short strips of rope and a few pairs of rusty pliers.

Keitel caught me looking at the table. "Ah, you see the pliers. We use those to crush knuckles. The ropes? You don't want to know what they're used for." His grin convinced me I was in the presence of evil.

I glanced away not wanting to think about what might happen in this room.

Two men stepped out of the kitchen. One had a huge white bandage on his nose. The other's walk was labored, his legs spread out. The chumps from Friday night. Not a welcome sight.

"Did you know they tried to rob me?" Gesturing toward the men, I looked at Hoermann.

Hoermann shook his head while Keitel looked at the two but said nothing.

I wanted to ask the one with the bandaged nose about his breathing and the one with the tender testicles about his sex life, but my 150 IQ suggested that wasn't a good idea, and I listened. No doubt they'd relish the opportunity for payback. I glanced at the pliers again. I had enough issues right now without antagonizing those melonheads. I smelled my own sweat, sure that everyone else could too. I must project strength, not weakness.

Couldn't expose my inner fear. I tried to clear my throat, but it was so dry I could barely swallow. "Can I have a glass of water?"

Keitel tipped his chin toward the man with the nose patch. "Get him some water." Then he moved behind me. "I'll uncuff you, but don't try anything foolish."

I heard a click and felt the steel binders detach. I flexed both wrists, the blood flow to my fingers slowly returning.

Nose Patch brought me a glass of water, but he slapped the back of my head before giving it to me. His way to get even. The urge to punch him back was hard to ignore.

I drank the cool liquid. All of it. Who knew if they'd give me any more?

Keitel slid into his chair, and the stiff-legged man brought over a manila envelope and set it on the table.

Hoermann studied both of us for a moment, then turned and walked out the door. Not that he'd been any help, but his leaving added to my growing anxiety.

Keitel opened the packet, pulled out a binder, then turned on the floodlight, directing the light at my face.

I lifted my hand to shield the glare. Sweat popped out on my forehead.

"Put your hand down and look at me." Keitel barked the order.

Obeying, I squinted but could barely see him.

The sound of pages flipping seemed deafening in the almost empty room. "Well, *Herr* Pepperman, you've had an interesting life. This information describes you as a very active young boy, participating in soccer, ice hockey, and boxing. You were also a good student, top of your class, but at times challenging. Fistfights with older boys. Teachers had to correct your disruptive behavior. You must have been a real thorn in their sides."

"Bullies." Still squinting, I tried to focus on him. "The older boys bullied my classmates, and I took up for them. Is that a crime?"

"Did you win most of those fights?" Surprisingly, there was a note of admiration in his voice.

"What do you think?"

His laughter echoed off the cold, dirty, bare walls. "I think you probably did."

Keitel's dossier about my life went on for a least an hour. The light never wavered from my face as sweat dripped down and off my chin. The Gestapo knew I'd only lost two boxing bouts from the time I was sixteen through college. They knew about all the medals I'd won. They knew about my father's brother Wilhelm moving to America.

Keitel took off his coat and rolled up his sleeves with his massive hands. "You visited with your Uncle Wilhelm and his son Patrick at the Olympic Games in Berlin."

"Yes."

"Your uncle works for the American government." He flipped the pages of the manual aggressively.

"No. He's an accountant."

"He's a spy." Keitel leaned in.

Could he not hear the truth in my voice? My eyes were tired. I rubbed them with my thumb and middle finger.

Keitel nodded toward one of the thugs.

My hands were yanked behind me and once again shackled. This time behind my head.

"We've tracked your uncle from London to Hamburg," Keitel said. "Do you communicate with him about your job?"

"*Nein*. I hardly correspond with him at all." Where was the Gestapo getting their information?

"Who do you talk with using the shortwave radio?" Keitel's voice ranged from very soft to very loud, his intimidation intensifying the interrogation.

"I told you the radio is not mine. Someone planted it in my room."

The questions lasted all day. Keitel alternated having me sit and stand. And the light, so close to my face, almost burned. Sweat ran to the end of my nose. Not being able to wipe my face was another form of torture. I shook my head to get rid of the water, but more kept coming.

My legs ached from my hips to my feet, the pain so severe it felt like bee stings, pulsating at times. I was a disciplined person, but my emotions were out of balance. Without balance, there was no sanity. And always, that *verdammt* light shined in my eyes. The only saving grace? The pliers and ropes remained on the table unused.

Keitel finally walked away from me.

I caught his silhouette staring out the window. I couldn't see Hoermann and the other two men, but I heard them moving behind me.

"Do you ever take work back to your hotel room?" Keitel asked, walking back to me.

"Yes." Fischer and his *dummkoph* ideas. I knew taking work out of the office wasn't allowed. Was that what landed me here on Keitel's interrogation chair accused as a Russian spy? It didn't even seem logical.

"Who do you share work secrets with?" Keitel continued his questions.

"No one. I've told you over and over that I'm not a spy." Irritation mixed with exhaustion tainted my voice. "I took work home because I cared about my responsibility. I'm serious about my job."

After a while, I couldn't concentrate on his questions. The temperature dropped with the sun, and I was so cold I shook, and all I could think about was sleep. Every time I dozed off, someone sprayed ice water in my face. I became disoriented, and I hallucinated about wild boars chasing me through the forest.

Somewhere in all of this, I heard the door open and saw the outlines of a few more men enter the room. One strode over to whisper something in Keitel's ear. Whatever was said changed his demeanor and made me think the man must be Keitel's superior. I don't know how long they stayed, but finally they filed out the door.

Fatigue settled in, and I pulled the plug on the chatter in my head. The questions and hallucinations and freezing water continued.

The sunrise came through the window three times before Keitel said to Hoermann, "Let's take him to another location. I'll get the car. You ride with him in the backseat."

This was it. They were done with me. Now that I had no value, they were going to kill me, and there was nothing I could do to stop them. Closing my eyes, I gave up the fight to stay awake.

"Hans, Hans, wake up." Someone lightly tapped me on the cheek. "Hans, can you hear me?"

Soft music was coming from somewhere. So weak I could barely raise my head, I opened my eyes to Hoermann's face blurring in and out of my vision.

"You've been asleep for twelve hours." Keitel leaned down on my other side and tugged on my shoulder. "Hans, can you hear me?"

Gasping for air, I let him help me sit up so I could look around. I was alive. And in a new place. The room was covered in faded floral wallpaper. There with empty spaces on the wall where pictures had once hung. The smell was different too. In place of urine and the metallic odor of dried blood, remnants of powder and perfume lingered. Maybe a woman's space. But one thing was for sure, there were no lights, pliers, or ropes. And the other two men were gone.

Hoermann smiled. He actually smiled and seemed relieved. "Are you okay?"

Keitel left and came back with a sandwich. "I know you are hungry." He handed me the plate. "Here, eat."

I glance around again. "You're not going to kill me?"

"We were never going to kill you," Hoermann said.

Hoping the food wasn't poisoned, I snatched the plate and took a bite of the sandwich, then another, and another. While still chewing, I asked. "Where am I?"

"You're in a house in Augsburg." Keitel had gone from impossible interrogator to normal person.

They let me finish my meal, and Hoermann brought me a glass of water. After he'd filled the glass twice more, I wiped my face with the back of my hand. Feeling stronger, I got down to business. "I want answers." I grabbed his sleeve.

He tried to pull it from my grip. "You've been through a lot." He attempted to soothe me with his tone.

It didn't work. "Oh, really." I gave him a glare and released his shirt.

Hoermann looked at Keitel, then back at me. "We know you're not a spy, but we had to make it look as though you were. "

"What?" I mustered as much rage as I possibly could.

"We have an idea who is stealing our secrets," Keitel said, "and we need you to set a trap for him. Will you help us?"

"Help you?" I focused all the contempt I was feeling at the man who seemed to have forgotten he'd tortured me for days. "After what you did to me?"

Keitel brought a chair to my bed and sat. "We had to make this look real in front of the other Gestapo agents because we can trust no one. I've applied sleep deprivation on a number of men, and everyone, except you, capitulated and told me what I wanted. You are one tough-minded bastard." His tone was congratulatory.

"Most people would have lied to stop the interrogation," Hoermann added, clearly proud I'd passed his insane test. "But you didn't crack. You are to be commended."

"That's because I had nothing to tell. If I had, I would have told you." Idiots. I wanted to scrub the floor with the two *trottels,* although I knew I was in no condition to do so.

While they continued to smile at me, I ran my hand over my head so I didn't use my fists on them. How had I gotten into this mess? Even more, how could I get out?

CHAPTER 27

der 27. März 1937
Augsburg, Germany

I FOUND PAPER IN THE HOUSE AT AUGSBURG. IT IS NOT MY journal, but it will have to do. Something about putting my life on paper helps me to sort it out. And right now, there is a lot to sort out. Messerschmitt had been in on Hoermann and Keitel's plan all along. Does that mean I am not fired? As for whatever Hoermann has next for me, all I know is this line of work is definitely against my calling. Unfortunately, I do not think I am going to have a choice but to follow through...

The sun had just gone down when I heard a vehicle pull up. Keitel and Hoermann had gone out for the afternoon and left me alone. I looked through the curtains and watched them walk around to the back of the house.

The squeaky, water-stained door opened, and they both entered through the kitchen. Hoermann raised his hands above his head, lifting four bottles of Grolsch lager *bier*. "For your enjoyment, Pepperman."

Keitel removed his black leather coat and draped it across a chipped wooden chair. "Is there anything else we can get you?"

"How about a razor?" I pointed to my stubbled whiskers. "And a change of clothes?" I tugged on my shirt.

"Not just yet. I'll explain later." Keitel put a brown briefcase on the table. *Click. Click.* Both latches flew open, and he pulled out a binder. Accepting the *bier* Hoermann handed him, he released the wire restraint, popped the cork, and took a big drink. When he set it on the table, foam gushed from the top.

Hoermann and I popped the corks on our own drinks. I lifted the bottle to my nose. Hops, barley, and yeast. It had been days since my last *bier*. I was going to thoroughly enjoy this delicious golden nectar before Keitel got down to business.

My opinion had not changed about the Gestapo agent. He was a loyal Nazi, and his political affiliations were twisted. I couldn't help but grin at Hoermann. But I didn't know how I could have been so wrong about the Abwehr Intelligence officer when I first met him in Baron's office in Stuttgart. He had appeared to be loyal to Hitler, but it was his country he truly loved.

Keitel opened the three-ringed binder. "With your boss's help, we've developed a plan to catch the suspected spy." He had trouble turning the flimsy pages with his large, vein-covered hands and big fingers.

I leaned forward. What he said piqued my interest. "You said a plan to catch the suspected spy. You must have a name."

Hoermann and Keitel looked at each other.

"We suspect two people," Keitel said.

"Who?" I asked.

Hoermann's sly smile seemed to indicate he knew. "One is a draftsman at the aircraft factory. He works in a different building, and you probably don't know him." There was a heavy pause. "The other" — he pulled on his earlobe — "is Ernst Fischer."

His words were slow to register. I leaned back in my chair, shocked. "You're joking, right?" No possible way Fischer was a traitor. I was a good judge of character. It had to be the draftsman.

"Do you think it was a coincidence Fischer was the one who found you the night you were attacked at the aircraft factory?" Hoermann asked.

"Here's what we know." Keitel's words were concise. "Shortwave transmissions have been coming from the apartment complex where Fischer and the other man live. But we can't pinpoint the exact location of the signals. This is where you come in, and why we can't get you a new set of clothes. You'll go to Fischer's apartment and tell him you escaped from the Gestapo and want to hide out a few days until you can leave Augsburg."

I turned my hands palms up. "What good will that do?"

Keitel lifted his hand. "You must let me finish. Messerschmitt knows you and Fischer are friends. He will ask Fischer to put your briefcase, the one you left next to Messerschmitt's desk, in your office."

"But why do I need to stay at his apartment?"

"I'm getting there." Keitel's voice took on some impatience.

Well, he definitely wouldn't like what I said next. "You should know I had schematics of the 109 in my briefcase, and I wasn't supposed to take work home."

"Yes, we know." Hoermann flipped his empty bottle in a trash can near the door. "Messerschmitt blew a gasket when he opened your briefcase. You'll have to answer for that later. But he did remove the blueprints. Because you're the only one who works on engine issues at the facility, Fischer won't suspect that you'll have left false information in the briefcase."

"And just what false information would I be leaving?"

"Anything that won't set off his alarm bells." Hoermann shrugged. "But something that will be interesting enough for him to share."

"If he's the spy." He couldn't be. But I'd do what they asked. "I'll jot down that the 109 fuel injection malfunctions after twelve hours and the injector needs to be redesigned." It seemed a plausible lie.

Hoermann grinned as he tapped his fingers together. "If we intercept a radio transmission stating the fuel injector needs to be redesigned, we'll know he's the spy."

I nodded. It was a clever plan. One that would let Fischer off the hook when he didn't take the bait. "When is all this going to take place?" I looked at both men.

"Write the note," Keitel said. "We'll give it to Messerschmitt tomorrow. He'll put it in your briefcase but won't have Fischer take it to your office until we know you're at his apartment."

"What if Fischer doesn't find the note or even go through my briefcase?"

"Then he's probably not a spy," Keitel said.

"Whose idea was this?" I crossed my arms, still not convinced.

Keitel pointed to Hoermann.

I wasn't surprised. Whatever physical qualities Hoermann lacked, his mind made up for. But not all of his plan made sense. "I still don't understand why you want me to stay with Fischer."

Hoermann took a handkerchief from his back pocket, blew his bulbous nose, then stuffed the soiled cloth into his pants. "While he's at work, you'll have plenty of opportunities to look for evidence."

"To clear him?"

"To catch him." Keitel countered

I shook my head slowly from side to side. "This is a waste of time."

Ignoring that last comment, Hoermann said, "After 10:00, we'll drive you within a couple of blocks of his apartment and drop you off."

"What if he's not willing to take me in?" I lowered my head.

"We'll hang back and see what happens. If he doesn't want you to stay, we'll pick you up and go with another plan." Taking a cigar from his shirt pocket, Hoermann held it at an angle. He struck a match and kept it near the end of the tobacco, rotating the cigar until it was lit. His first draw seemed slow and controlled. After a few seconds, he tilted his head back and gently blew out a large puff of smoke.

The smell reminded me of the first time I met him. "What's the other plan?"

He scratched his throat with his stubby fingers. "I'm working on it."

"So, you have no other plan," I said.

As if he hadn't heard me, he walked out of the room and back to the kitchen.

When we left the house, we stepped into a moonless night. A loose shutter banged against the side of the house, wind whistled through the trees, and branches bent and scraped against the roof. I'd been reading Poe in my spare time. All the images of his stories stuck in my head.

I started to shake, not from the cold but from the unknown. I buttoned my coat and lifted the collar to block the wind. We walked to the front of the house, and I drew in several noisy breaths. I spat on the ground, then jammed the spit into the grass with the heel of my shoe before getting into the car. Just thinking about what I was about to do angered me.

As promised, Hoermann and Keitel dropped me a couple of blocks from Fischer's apartment.

A car turned the corner onto his street. Anna's car. I ducked behind a tree until the vehicle passed, warmth spreading up my arms into my heart. I wanted so much to see her. I watched her car until she turned into her building area and disappeared, my longing for her undeniable. Would I ever see her again? Did she know about my arrest? If she did, would she ever look at me again the way she used to? Could we have the same relationship?

Letting those thoughts go for now, I crossed the street. The curtains in Fischer's living room were opened, and I saw him inside dancing around, flipping his arms in an awkward motion.

I let out a quiet chuckle. It didn't seem possible he could be a traitor.

Raising a closed fist to the door, I rapped twice, wondering what he thought of me being a spy and if he'd even invite me in, let alone let me stay.

He opened the door, mouth parting, and adjusted his glasses. "Hans, what are you doing here?" He grabbed my arm, pulled me inside, shut the door, then locked it.

"Thank you for letting me in."

He rushed to the window and pulled the curtains shut. "What's going on? I've been worried about you."

Could I do this? Could I lie to my friend? Yes, because that was how I was going to clear him. I bolstered myself up inside to play the role I had to. "The Gestapo's been interrogating me." I let all my earlier fear from when I'd been arrested show in my eyes. "I managed to escape. You're the only one I can trust."

Concern for me growing in his face, he pointed to the couch. "Sit, let's talk. Can I get you something to eat or drink?"

"Yes, please." I plopped down hard, feeling all the weight of what I was about to do. "I haven't eaten in two days."

After getting me some roasted chicken and a glass of water, he sat in a chair across from the couch. Thank goodness he didn't offer that gosh-awful sausage he loved.

"Why did they arrest you?"

I chewed and swallowed a bite of chicken. "Someone hid a shortwave radio under my bed at the hotel. The Gestapo searched my room and found it. They think I'm leaking secret military information."

"That's insane." His rested his hands on his hips. "Who do you think is trying to set you up?"

My hands shook so hard I had difficulty handling the food. Lying will do that to an honest person. "I don't know, and I don't want to get you in trouble. If you'll let me spend the night and stay the next day, I'll leave. But I need rest."

"Of course. Stay as long as you want." His tone was sincere, just as I'd expected.

"Have you seen Anna?" Just thinking about her saddened me. I longed to touch her soft skin and smell the wonderful fragrance of her hair.

"Yes. She knows the Gestapo picked you up, and she's upset. Do you want to see her?" He moved to stand.

"*Nein. Nein.*" I gestured for him to sit back down. "I can't get her involved, and I'm putting you at risk just by being here."

"Don't worry about me. This is so crazy. I know you could never do anything to betray Germany."

I hoped I wasn't doing anything to betray him. "Look, Fischer, I —"

Knock. Knock.

I sprang off the couch, tensing.

"Quick. Into my bedroom. Shut the door." Fischer's voice was soft but urgent. "I'll get rid of them."

I hurried to his bedroom and cracked the door so I could see.

He straightened the sofa cushion, rushed my plate of half-eaten chicken into the kitchen, and ran back out. He paused, composing himself, before opening the door. "Heidi, how good to see you."

She walked in, and he shut the door.

"It sounded like you were talking to someone." Heidi pushed her wind-blown hair from her face.

Fischer laughed, but it didn't sound normal. "*Nein.* I was talking to myself. I often do that when I'm having a problem with my work. It helps me break up the cobwebs in my mind."

Heidi stood by the door, her arms crossed as if she were cold. "Do you have any more news about Hans? What has the Gestapo done with him? Anna's worried sick."

Fischer motioned to the sofa. "Please sit. I'll tell you what I know."

She shook her head. "Anna called crying. I'm on my way to see her."

"The people at the aircraft factory said Hans was a spy."

"Do *you* think he's guilty?" Heidi's tone was low. Concerned.

"He's not the type to betray his country." The way Fischer stood up for me only made me more determined to prove to Hoermann and Keitel that he was innocent.

"So sad." She shifted from side to side. "I thought I'd check to see if you had any information."

"Anna works at the Gestapo office. I would think she'd know something," Fischer said.

Heidi shrugged. "I asked her. Nothing was discussed in her department."

Fischer cupped a hand over his mouth. "This doesn't look good. But I will never believe Hans would be a traitor to his country."

Heidi took a deep breath and exhaled, then took Fischer's hands in hers. "I don't know what to do to help Anna. I'm sorry to rush, but she's expecting me. Please let me know if you hear anything."

"Yes, of course." He kissed her cheek. "Give my best to Anna."

After he shut the door, I walked into the living room.

He peeked through the curtains, watching her leave. "Are you sure you don't want me to tell Anna you're okay?"

"*Nein. Nein.* I told you, I don't want her in the middle of this."

Fischer nodded. "Of course, you're right." He looked at me and grinned. "Changing the subject, you could use a fresh shirt and a good shower."

I laughed. "I don't think your shirt would fit, but I'll take you up on that shower."

He patted me on the shoulder. "I can take care of that, my friend." He went to the bathroom, laid out a towel, wash cloth, and a bar of soap. "When you're finished, you can have my bed for tonight. I'll sleep on the couch."

"That's not necessary."

"Nonsense. You sleep well, and I won't wake you in the morning. You need rest." He walked out of his bedroom and shut the door.

Just thinking about searching the apartment made me sick. The shower wasn't going to fix my feelings, but it would wash the stink off my body. After enjoying the hot water far too long, I dried and went to bed.

The next morning, after I heard Fischer leave for work, I stayed in bed a good half hour, not wanting to do what I had to do. Finally, I pulled back the covers, dressed in the same filthy clothes, tried to ignore the stench, and went into the kitchen.

Fischer had left a note on the table.

There is a large slice of apple strudel in the refrigerator. Help yourself to the sausage and cheese for lunch. I will see you after work.

His kindness added to my guilt, but the thought of eating that repulsive sausage made me gag.

After breakfast, I started the search. I checked his bedside table — a pair of glasses, one copy of the newspaper *Der Stürmer*, and photos his mama wouldn't approve of. They weren't pictures I'd look at either. But Fischer could do what Fischer wanted.

I lifted the bedspread and looked under the bed next and found a shotgun. If he were a hunter, that would surprise me. My guess? The weapon was for protection. Luckily, I didn't find a shortwave radio. A good sign. That was what I'd been concerned with the most.

The closet was next. I flipped through hangers of slacks, dress coats, and shirts. At the far back, I saw three dresses — one with bright yellow flowers, another with blue and white stripes, and the last a dirndl. Odd? Heidi's? Or Fischer's mother's?

Several hat boxes lined the shelves above the hanging clothes. I reached up and lifted the tops off the boxes. Inside were women's wigs in blonde, black, and brown.

Now I understood the photos. And I began to see Fischer in a different light. If the pictures didn't drive his mother over the edge, the dresses would. As for me, I didn't care. What he did in his private life was his business. He was still a good friend.

The last place I searched was his dresser. I looked in his sock drawer and discovered a metal object I didn't recognize stuffed into a sock. I pulled it out and held it up, studying the two dials, number calibrations, and the depression button in the center. Shrugging, I stuffed it back where I found it — an odd place to conceal an instrument. But then, Fischer was turning out to *be* a little odd. I closed the drawer. Not wanting to be here when he returned, I left him a note thanking him for his kindness and called the number Keitel had given me.

He told me to meet him in thirty minutes in a wooded area behind Fischer's place.

The sky was overcast and misty as I waited. The dreariness depressed me, and the chill caused me to shiver

At 3:00 p.m., Keitel arrived at the pickup point.

I opened the car door and slid in, blowing on my cupped hands to warm them. "Where's Hoermann?"

Keitel turned the car around and headed back to the house. "He's working on a project. Do you have any helpful information?"

I shrugged. "Not sure. Let's wait until we get back. I still think you suspect the wrong man." At least I hoped so.

We arrived at the house about twenty minutes later, when the heavy mist had turned into a shower. The windshield wipers made a soft whooshing sound as they scraped across the glass. We waited in his vehicle until several cars passed before hurrying to the back door.

Hoermann had papers spread all over the kitchen table and the countertops. He was good at his job, but his organization and neatness needed some work. "How was your night, Hans?" He never looked up from his clutter.

"Good." Despicable me. I'd hated invading Fischer's privacy.

Looking over the top of his half-frame glasses, Hoermann pushed away from the table and stood. "Let's go to the living room." He sat in a large-cushioned arm-chair with faded floral print marred with split seams.

I sat on the ugly brown couch. Like the chair, the sofa had seen better days.

Keitel brought a chair from the kitchen.

"Well, what do you have for us?" Hoermann linked his fingers together and rested his hands on his portly stomach.

They weren't going to like what I had to say. I crossed my legs, resting my arm along the top of the sofa. "No shortwave radio. Nothing that would incriminate him."

Hoermann glanced at Keitel. The disappointing looks they gave each other said it all. "If no transmission is done in a few days concerning the problem with the fuel injection system, we'll have to concentrate our efforts on the draftsman. Are you sure there isn't something?"

I wasn't going to tell either of them about the dresses or wigs. I couldn't do that to Fischer. I shook my head, then remembered something I could say. "There was an instrument about the size of a small cigar stuffed into one of his socks." Then I went on to describe it in more detail.

Hoermann sprang from his chair, hurried into the kitchen, and returned. "Did it look like this?" He held up an item identical to what I'd found.

"Yes, exactly like that."

Hoermann slapped his thighs, then his knees, and tried to slap the sole of his shoe attempting to do a tradi-tional Bavarian folk dance. Finally giving up, he looked at me. "Do you know what this is, Hans?"

CHAPTER 28

der 28. März 1937
Augsburg, Germany

IT IS NICE TO HAVE MY JOURNAL BACK. MY CLOTHES AND TRUNK,
along with the rest of my possessions, have been moved here.
That means I will not be going back to the hotel any time soon.
Or maybe ever.

Hoermann thinks the gadget in Fischer's sock drawer is a
subminiature spy camera, so small that Hoermann could hide
it in his fist. If he is right, that means Fischer's probably taking
photos of top-secret aircraft schematics. Though I am still not
totally convinced he is the spy. Or maybe it is just that I do
not want him to be. I am tired. I need to sleep...

"Wake up. We have news." Hoermann stood in my
doorway, his tone peppered with excitement.

I rubbed my eyes and looked at my watch. 9:00. I'd
slept five hours. "What's going on?"

"Come with me." He didn't wait for my reply.

I got up, slipped on my shoes, and followed him to
the kitchen.

Hoermann's cluttered mess had doubled. Even the
kitchen chairs were crammed to overflowing.

"We've heard from the intelligence service. A transmission was picked up tonight," Keitel said.

"And?" My heart almost stopped beating. The news could mean only one thing. Part of me didn't want to hear it.

"Fischer took the bait. He sent out a transmission about the fuel injector." Hoermann removed his reading glasses and looked at me as if he were waiting for me to add the punch line to a joke.

Without intending to, I obliged. "He's the spy."

Hoermann nodded.

Fischer was selling out Germany? How could he hate his countrymen so much he'd betray them? Why? I rubbed the enlarged knuckle on my right hand. Why would he do that? Did he think he was rescuing us from Germany's leadership or was he being blackmailed? "When are you going to arrest him?"

"Not now. He may have an accomplice." Keitel moved some paper stacks from a chair and sat, stretching out his legs. Locking his fingers behind his head, he said *I told you so* without using a word.

"If we pick him up, his partner will most likely leave the country," Hoermann explained.

"What makes you think he has an accomplice?" I cupped a hand over my eyes and rubbed. Things were not looking good for Fischer.

"Russian spies work in pairs." Keitel straightened and set his heavy hands on his knees. His deep-set eyes belonged to a medieval executioner with an axe. "If he's been taking photos, someone could be helping him get those films out of the country."

I swallowed hard as if that would get the bad taste out of my mouth. "And into Russia?" Would Fischer do that for money? He didn't seem materialistic.

Both Hoermann and Keitel nodded.

"How will you catch the other spy?" I asked.

Hoermann peered over his half-spectacles, his eyebrows resembling slanting twigs. "We will continue to follow Fischer and concentrate on the restaurants and bars he frequents." He cleared his throat, looking like now he had a bad taste in his mouth. "We believe he's a transvestite." Shifting, he cleared his throat again. "Anyway" — he waved his hand in dismissal — "We know the places they gather. We'll film his every move. And hopefully, he'll lead us to his accomplice."

The photos in his bedside table and the dresses in the closet made sense now. How long had the Gestapo known about Fischer's personal habits? I guess it really didn't matter. "What can I do to help?"

"Once we have the films developed, we'll need you to see if you recognize anyone he's with." Hoermann shrugged. "It's a long shot, but who knows? The filming could be successful."

"What's your plan to film Fischer?"

"We've rented building spaces across from his apartment and his favorite bars and restaurants. We're not letting him out of our sight," Keitel said.

"What made you suspect Fischer?" I asked. That still bothered me. Why hadn't I noticed anything peculiar? Shouldn't I have?

Hoermann tugged on his forever drooping pants. "The night you and Fischer were attacked at the aircraft factory, he said he got to the plant after 11:00. I checked the register at the gate, and he logged in at 9:37. His lie made me suspicious. He may have been the one who jumped you and injured himself to make it look like he was attacked. We've tracked him ever since."

My life was unraveling at both ends. My friend, who turned out to be a traitor to the Fatherland, was assisting Russia, a country that committed civil atrocities against its own people. Europe appeared to be rushing into war. My trust in people slowly withered like old wallpaper, curling and twisting away from the wall.

None of this made sense. None of it.

CHAPTER 29

der 10. April 1937
Augsburg, Germany

BEING COOPED UP FOR THE LAST TWO WEEKS HAS BEEN TEDIOUS. But at least Messerschmitt allows Hoermann to bring my work from the office. The 109 engine keeps me busy when we are not watching the films taken of Fischer. We have been over them so many times looking for the smallest clue as to who is helping him. I have not recognized anyone going into his apartment or the businesses he frequents. When I suggested the drafts-man at the aircraft factory as the other spy, Hoermann said that man had been cleared.

During breaks, Keitel challenges us to games of poker, bet-ting matchsticks. Poor Hoermann does not even have a match left to light his cigar. He and I are becoming good friends as we struggle to discover Fischer's accomplice...

I was sitting at the kitchen table going over the blue-prints of the fuel injector when Hoermann burst through the backdoor.

Tilting his head back, he looked out from under those gnarly eyebrows, his dark, deep-set eyes full of anger. "This *verdammt* winter weather must end. It's almost the middle of April, and this snow is driving me insane. Another arctic blast is headed our way tomorrow."

I grinned at the mostly amiable comrade. "Why are you angry at me? I didn't bring the weather."

Hoermann's temper caused him to sweat and intensified his body odor. He set his briefcase next to the sink and softly chuckled. "It's not you, my friend. My apologies."

Keitel followed him into the kitchen, unbuttoned his coat and laid it on the countertop. "He's been this way all day. His bitching and moaning remind me of a constipated geriatric in need of an enema."

I laughed, got up from the table, and grabbed Hoermann's arm. "I'll hold him down. Keitel, get the warm water ready."

"Stop, Hans, you burly bastard. You're making me laugh, and I'll piss myself. Get me a *bier*," Hoermann commanded.

I turned him loose and gently jabbed his right shoulder. "A *bier* it is."

Keitel had already opened the refrigerator, pulled out three bottles, and popped the lids.

Hoermann yanked a wadded handkerchief from his back pocket, blew his nose, and then belched. He looked at Keitel first, then me. His puffy lips straightened. "See what you made me do." He wiped his mouth with the same cloth. "Is the projection screen set up in the living room?" He pointed his *bier* bottle at me.

I nodded.

"Keitel, get the projector ready. I'm going to answer Mother Nature."

While Hoermann took care of business, I helped Keitel thread the film. "What's the location of this roll?"

"The Reigele Wirsthaus restaurant last Saturday." Keitel flipped off the overhead light just as Hoermann came in and took his usual seat in the faded armchair.

The projector flickered, sending images across the screen of Fischer approaching the restaurant. He met a lady on the street, shook her hand, and spoke a few words before walking away.

I grabbed Keitel's arm and shook it hard. "Run that back again." I asked him to repeat that process two more times.

"Do you see something?" Hoermann's voice arched as though the anticipation was more than he could stand.

"Can you pull out the previous film of Fischer at this restaurant?" Had Fischer and the woman exchanged something? Maybe film? And was that really a woman — or a man dressed as a woman?

Keitel turned on the overhead light and laced an earlier tape of the Reigele Wirsthaus. As it played, the projector heated up, the smell reminding me of an over-baked chocolate cake.

The scene was almost identical to the most recent. The same woman wearing the same coat met Fischer on the street in front of the restaurant. Again they shook hands and talked briefly.

A *thump, thump, thumping* started in my head, and I peered harder at the screen.

The projector clattered over the wind slamming the shutters against the side of the house.

I made Keitel play it one more time, then I got up and walked out of the room. It felt like I was trudging through mud.

Someone grabbed my arm and turned me around.

Hoermann. His eyes, so close to mine, looked out of focus. "What is it, Hans? What did you see?"

A massive rage escalated inside me. A different kind of rage than when I boxed. I had no animosity for my opponents in the ring. But this feeling was different. I wanted revenge. I looked Hoermann in the eye. "I know who it is."

CHAPTER 30

June 1999
Bartlesville, Oklahoma

AFTER READING HANS'S LIFE ALOUD TO LAURA FOR THREE hours, my voice needed a rest. I set the journal on the table by my chair and stretched.

"Why are you stopping, Jim?" Laura sat up from where she'd been lounging on the couch across the room. "Keep going." She clutched the glass of iced tea she'd been nursing and leaned forward. "I have to know."

Getting comfortable again, I opened the journal, just as eager to see who he'd recognized on the film.

But the next page was blank.

What? That couldn't be right. I sat straighter and turned the next page.

Still nothing.

I licked my thumb and flipped through the rest of the pages. They fluttered like cards being shuffled, the sound hollow, the paper void of words. All that greeted me was the musty smell of an old book.

"Jim, keep reading." Laura's tone was in no way a request.

Setting the open journal on my lap, I shook my head. "That's all." I'd given three hours of my life to Hans's journal—and now nothing. It was like being enthralled in an epic movie that was permanently paused during intermission. The blank pages felt like a promise made but not kept. I needed to know what happened.

"What do you mean, that's all?" Laura set her glass on the table and swung her feet to the floor, her face etched with disappointment.

"I mean, that's all. There's nothing else to read." Exasperated, I slapped the arm of my chair.

Laura sprang off the couch, hurried over, and picked up the journal. She flipped through the pages like she could magically make the rest of the story appear. "There's nothing else."

"That's what I said."

She gingerly closed the old book and exhaled a frustrated burst of air. "We've got to find out who Hans saw in the film." She put a hand over her mouth as if to hold back curse words screaming to escape. "What are we going to do? Hans can't leave us hanging like this." She broke into a childlike grin, realizing Hans had no idea he'd left us hanging and didn't care.

I matched her smile. "What do you want me to do? Call and scold him for leaving us in the dark."

"Yes. That is exactly what I want you to do." Her precise tone left no doubt what she wanted.

"What?"

"We've got to find out if he's still living." She held the journal next to her chest, her voice stern. "We've got to find out what happened."

I did the math in my head. "Hans was in his twenties in 1937. He'd be in his mideighties now."

Laura put the journal on the table. "We have to find him. We have to try."

"But where do we start?"

She bit down on her lower lip. "I'll do a search on our Gateway computer. Let's start with Augsburg, Germany."

"It's worth a try." My heart pounded with the possibility of discovering a part of my family's history that had been lost. But could it be done? "Germany invaded Poland in 1939, over sixty years ago. If World War II didn't kill him, attrition could have. What are the chances of locating him even if he's alive?"

Suddenly, nothing else mattered but to discover what had happened to this fascinating man and to learn the story of his life. We had to find Hans.

CHAPTER 31

July 1999
Bartlesville, Oklahoma

THE PAST FEW WEEKS I'D ESPECIALLY LOOKED FORWARD TO getting home from work to see what Laura's research had uncovered. The possibility of finding Hans constantly on my mind, I set my briefcase on the kitchen counter and walked to the computer room to find her staring at the computer screen.

The computer desk was strewn with loose papers and yellow sticky notes. Empty soda cups filled the trash can by the door, and crumpled Dove candy bar wrappers dotted the desk.

She'd spent two weeks searching for Hans. Her efforts had found a number of Peppermans in Augsburg and his hometown Hamburg, Germany, but none that panned out. I couldn't stop wondering what he looked like, if there was a family resemblance, and what he remembered about Dad coming to see him at the Olympic Games. I tried not to dwell on the fact that Hans might not be alive.

Laura took off her reading glasses and rubbed her eyes.

I stepped closer and touched her shoulder.

She flinched and turned toward me. "Oh, I didn't hear you come in." The tired look on her face told me all I needed to know.

"No luck?" I massaged her tense shoulders, the tightness loosening with each squeeze.

"No, and I'll give you thirty minutes to stop what you're doing." She closed her eyes, seeming to enjoy the attention, then set her hand on mine.

I gently lifted her arm, guiding her out of the chair. "Let's go to the living room."

She took her usual place on the sofa while I sat across from her in my chair.

I noticed a small crack in the glass of the large picture window behind her, probably from a hail stone. "Maybe this is not to be." I reached down, untied my shoes, and kicked them to the side.

Laura sat, crossing her legs. "I don't know what else to do. Our computer is so limited."

I hesitated, angling my head to the side. "What did you just say?"

"I said I don't know what else I can do."

"No, about the computer."

She shrugged her shoulders. "Our computer is limited on what it can do."

I threw back my head, looked at the ceiling, then back at her. "Why didn't I think of this before?"

She gave me a puzzled look. "Think of what before?"

I extended both arms straight out. "Sybil Adams."

Another confused look. "Sybil who?"

"Sybil Adams. She owns the company that installed our computers at work. She's a retired Army colonel.

Maybe she has contacts in the military that can help us find Hans."

Laura grinned and uncrossed her legs. "Do you think the government computers are capable of doing a little more than ours?" Her facetious tone was obvious.

I nodded. "I'd bet on it."

"How soon can you talk with this lady?" Her speech accelerated.

"I'll try tomorrow. The home office of Systems, Inc. is in Tulsa."

"Do you think she'll remember you?"

"I'm sure of it. I was on the committee explaining what we needed from their computers. I worked directly with her."

Laura sat on the edge of the couch, leaning forward. "This could be the break we've been looking for. I've got one question."

"What's that?"

"Why didn't you think of this two weeks ago?" She picked up a sofa pillow and playfully chunked it my way.

I caught the cushion and laid it next to my chair. "Let's think ahead. What if Sybil finds Hans? What do we do next?"

"What are you thinking?"

I could see the wheels in her head spinning, wondering where my thoughts were. "We call him, of course. If he's willing, would you want to go to Germany, if that's where he's living?"

"Jim, do you know how many years you've promised me a vacation to Europe?"

"No, but I think you do."

"It was before the triplets were born, and they are now fourteen."

"So, I'm a little bit late." I laughed and tossed the pillow back to her.

Laura didn't even try catching it. She just batted it away from her face and sat back, covering her mouth with her hands, tearing up. She dropped her hands and rubbed her thighs. "Can you imagine having a conversation with him? I feel as though I know this wonderful man already. His journal captivated me, and I have to find out what happened to him. I know you must feel the same way."

I looked at Laura, unable to answer her immediately. I swallowed hard and took several deep breaths. "I do." It wasn't just that I wanted to find Hans. I *had* to see him. I couldn't live with myself if I didn't do everything in my power to find this lost link to my heritage. "I'll call Sybil tomorrow."

The rest of the evening was mostly silent between the two of us. I believed her thoughts were on Hans. I knew mine were.

Laura went to bed before I did. She rested on her side, asleep.

I turned off the bedside light and slid under the covers. The house was quiet. All I heard from outside was the faint bark of a dog. I tried to think about what Hans's life must have been like during the war. I had no idea of the sufferings of the German people. The vast majority of the citizens were good, hard-working people just caught up in an evil regime.

At that moment, I felt warm and relaxed, sensing Hans Pepperman was alive. I smiled. Now the question was, could we find him?

CHAPTER 32

July 1999
Bartlesville, Oklahoma

THREE DAYS HAD PASSED SINCE MY CONVERSATION WITH SYBIL. At first, she'd been hesitant about helping Laura and me find Hans. The Army frowned on using their resources for personal reasons. But Sybil did have one contact who owed her a favor.

Right before I left my office, she called with news. Hurrying home, I couldn't wait to share what she'd learned. Bursting through the garage door, I set my briefcase on the kitchen counter. "Where are you, Laura?"

Smiling, she came out of the laundry room carrying a basketful of clean clothes. With her hair tied back with a red bandana and her face covered in a light green paste, I only saw the whites of her eyes and a bunch of white teeth.

"What in the heck have you got on your face?" I shook my head, not really wanting to know. "Never mind. Have a seat. I have good news and bad news."

"About Hans?" She put the basket on the floor, went to the living room, and sat in my lounge chair.

Nodding, I barely waited for her rear to hit the seat cushion before the good news erupted out. "I heard from Sybil today."

She straightened in the chair. "Okay." Her voice spiked with enthusiasm.

"Sybil found Hans."

Laura jumped out of the chair, both arms in the air. "Yes… Yes… Yes." Her bare feet pitter patted on the carpet as she sang, "Na na na na, hey hey, good news."

I thought she'd flipped her ever-loving mind. "Hold on." I pointed to the chair as I sat on the couch. "I might be ahead of myself." I cleared my throat and started again. "We may have found Hans."

Laura's shoulders slumped as she sat back down, her energy gone. "Go on."

"Sybil located a man in Munich fitting Hans's description. The only data the Army found is from five years back. The man was eighty-one at the time, which would make him eighty-six now. A lot can happen in five years. All we can do is hope. But hope is better than nothing."

"So that's the bad news? He might be dead?" She leaned forward.

"Well, that would be bad, but the other bad news is there's no phone number. But there is an address. *Arnulfstr* 2, apartment 312, not far from the Marienplatz, the center of Munich."

Laura scratched her cheek, forgetting the green goo on her face. She wiped her fingers on her jeans. "What do you want to do?"

"Go to Munich. What say you?"

Laura jammed both hands on her hips and rocked her head from side to side. "Not yes… but H-E-double toothpicks yes."

I couldn't help but grin at her corny cliché. "I'm scheduled to be off the next two weeks. The boys' All-Star baseball tournament is week after next. We can still go to Europe and be back in time for the tournament. But the boys can't go with us because of practice."

Laura dragged her hand across her mouth and down her chin, scrapping off more green goo. "Why don't we ask the Sturners if the boys can stay with them? Levi is on the team too."

"Great idea. If one of our boys gets a toothache, Dr. Jane's right there for him."

Laura rocked back in the chair. "And if one of them gets a cut, Dr. Dustin can do the sutures."

We both laughed.

"It's wonderful to have neighbors who are both doctors," I said.

Laura shook her head. "Poor little Ashley. With our three boys and her brother in one house for a week, she may not talk to us again."

I tried to temper my excitement, but it didn't work. We were about to leave our kids for at least a week to search for a man who may be my second cousin. Was I being too optimistic? Perhaps.

The odds were not in my favor that the Hans Pepperman in Munich was a relative. But I'd be damned if I wasn't going to find out.

CHAPTER 33

July 1999
Bartlesville, Oklahoma
Munich, Germany

PLANE RESERVATIONS WERE BOOKED. THE STURNERS HAD agreed to keep the triplets, and I hoped we'd still be friends after our return from Munich.

Feeling like a senior looking forward to his last prom night, I was excited about the possibility of locating Hans. As silly as that sounded, connecting the dots to my family history became extremely important to me.

When the plane made its final approach to Franz Josef Strauss International Airport in Munich, I looked at Laura staring intently out the window. "You're in deep thought. What about?"

She adjusted herself in the tight airplane seat. "I feel as though I'm going on my first date."

"Are you serious? That's a bit juvenile, don't you think?" I gave her a look of disbelief but chuckled to myself. No way was I going to tell her my feelings almost exactly matched hers.

By the time we picked up our luggage and fell into a taxi, it was 10:30 p.m. Exhausted, we missed most of what I was sure was a magnificent view as we drove to the Kempinski Hotel.

Laura turned on the seat to face me. "The Glockenspiel is a giant mechanical working clock in the Marienplatz with life-sized wooden figures that spin, telling two different sixteenth- century stories. A must-see while we're here."

I nodded. She was going to make the most of this trip. I should have taken her to Europe fifteen years ago like I'd promised.

At the hotel, we pulled our luggage down a long, elegant hallway with pale yellow walls and light green carpet. When we got to our room, I unlocked the door to a large, luxurious space. The bed, covered with a white spread, lush green pillows, and a dark green throw folded neatly at the foot, beckoned me. I sat on the firm mattress and breathed out a relaxing sigh. We'd made it. We were here.

The way Laura's shoulders dropped and her face smoothed out told me she felt the same. Tired from the flight and the time change, we took quick showers and went to bed. Neither of us could sleep. After we both tossed and turned for thirty minutes, Laura sat up and flipped on the bedside lamp. "My mind's a runaway freight train."

I fluffed my pillow and faced her. "My brain's a mess. I'm wondering if he's the right Hans. And if he is, will he want to see us? I can't imagine he wouldn't, but you never know. A man of his age may have become bitter with World War II and all he had to deal with. I want so much to get to know him. But even if he's interested in filling us in on his life, how much will he remember?"

Laura touched my cheek. "I have a good feeling we made the right decision. We'll find Hans, and he will love telling us about his life. This was meant to be. I just know it. Let's go to sleep and be ready for a good day. No. A great day." She kissed me on the check, then switched off the light.

Pulling her close, I hoped she was right. But I had my doubts, and as I watched the clock on the bedside table tick off the minutes toward morning, my spirits waned by the hour. We'd traveled thousands of miles to meet someone who might turn out not to be the someone we needed to find. How could we be so foolish to trust a gut feeling? I sighed and turned over again. At least we would know soon.

The alarm went off a few hours later, and Laura jumped out of bed and opened the curtains. "Jim, it's time to get up. This is going to be a fantastic day."

With my hand, I shielded my eyes from the bright light and rolled over to my stomach.

She flung the covers off me and slapped my backside. "Move it, big guy."

How did she have that much energy after our long flight? She must be on an adrenaline high.

I pulled the covers back over me. "You get ready first." My *you get ready first* was as pleasant sounding as I could make it. I wasn't nearly as excited about what the day would bring, but I didn't want to dampen her enthusiasm.

We ate breakfast at the hotel restaurant. The high-back, padded chairs and white linen tablecloths exuded style.

The staff wore white starched shirts and black pants. One filled our glasses with water, but there was no ice. That seemed odd.

In the front of the room, chefs in tall, pleated, starched hats were busy arranging food in an appetizing fashion on buffet tables filled with trays of fresh bread, butter, jam, honey, thinly sliced meats, cheese, and boiled eggs. Not exactly the pancakes and ham Laura would make on a Saturday morning. But this Saturday morning I was in Germany, and the aroma of the bread piqued my appetite.

I set the black zippered binder where I kept Hans's journal on the floor next to my chair and enjoyed a healthy breakfast. Then Laura and I walked a few blocks to the Marienplatz. I carried the journal in my right hand, protecting it as though it were a literary piece. My wife's enthusiasm had finally caught up to me, giving me a glimmer of hope about what this day could bring.

We passed a woman dressed in a maroon dirndl with a pink apron pushing a flower cart filled with red poppies, light purple roses, and yellow irises. The clean fragrance reminded me of a botanical garden. I could almost see cows grazing on the mountainside pastures.

Besides the usual vacationers wandering the streets, a group of people were preparing for what looked like some sort of race. There must have been at least a hundred participants. Some wore matching shorts and T-shirts. A few men wore Speedos and no shirts. And a couple of the women's shorts looked like Speedos, and they may as well have had on no shirt.

Laura laughed and put her hand over my eyes. "You're too young to see such things."

If only. I chuckled.

Moving her hands away from my face, Laura pointed at a large banner hanging between two light poles over where the runners gathered.

"*Bürgermeisterin* Linda Schallison's Annual 10K Run for Mental Illness," I read.

"Now that is an excellent cause." She gave me a not-so-gentle nudge. "What does *Bürgermeisterin* mean?"

"*Bürgermeisterin* is a female mayor. Linda Schallison is the mayor of Munich."

The starter pistol went off, and the bunched-up runners slowly moved forward.

I touched Laura on the shoulder. "Let's head on over to *Arnulfstr*. It's not far." My heartrate doubled, almost bringing me to my knees. What would my cousin look like? Part of me wanted to turn around and go back to the hotel, not wanting to face the disappointment of being let down if he wasn't our Hans.

As though Laura could read my mind, she grabbed my arm and gave it a squeeze. "It's okay. We can face this together." She shook her head. "This day will not be a disappointment."

Her smile settled me down. I knew she wanted this Hans to be the right Hans too.

As we walked to *Arnulfstr* 2, Laura pointed out the striking old Gothic architecture with rounded archways and tall spirals on top of the cold, gray stone buildings. She'd done her research preparing for this trip. But that was nothing new for her.

A bell in a tower up ahead clanged straight out of a scene from *The Hunchback of Notre Dame*. Although the story had taken place in another country, I could almost see the peasants milling around the stately church we were about to pass.

"Munich is famous for its Renaissance cathedrals and opulent royal palaces dating back to the twelfth century," Laura said.

"I can almost feel Hitler delivering a rousing speech about the Fatherland. The master orator duped most of the German people. Germany was a great country ruled by a maniacal dictator."

Too taken in by the charm of the old city, Laura didn't even hear me.

The walk seemed short. Before I knew it, we were in front of Hans's building. The ultra-modern apartment complex looked totally out of place among the other historic buildings that so characterized Munich.

Laura tapped her forehead with her palm. "I wonder what bird-brained architect put this twentieth-century structure right in the middle of this beautiful town."

I paused. Not over the garishness of the modern architecture. Over the fact that this was our moment of truth.

Laura had none of my hesitancy. She took my hand, led me through a pair of glass doors across the lobby to the elevator, and pushed the up button.

As the soft, powerful motor lifted us, a hideous, high-pitched beep signaled each floor and made me cringe. Finally, the metal door opened on the third level.

Laura and I looked at each other. Her eyes danced like those of a child about to enter a candy store.

For me, stepping out of that elevator felt like walking into a funeral home. I hoped that wasn't a bad omen.

Laura pointed to the arrow on the wall indicating 312 would be the hallway to the left. Our steps echoed down the long, empty corridor until we reached the door.

I looked at Laura again. I thought I was going to have to grab her arm to keep her from floating to the ceiling. What was she thinking?

A mass of excitement jumbled with fear ran through my head. The fear of the unknown was the worst. If the door opened, what would I say? How would I react if this Hans *was* my cousin? How would I react if he *wasn't*?

I felt like a belt was strapped around my chest, yanked to the last notch, squeezing all the air out of my lungs. Hans's journal trembled in my hand. Putting it behind my back, I held tight to the binding to keep from shaking.

Our decision to come was based on a Hans Pepperman living at this address five years ago. What were the chances of him still residing here?

We were about to find out.

Squaring my shoulders, I lifted my fist and knocked twice.

CHAPTER 34

July 1999
Munich, Germany

AFTER THE THIRD UNANSWERED KNOCK AT APARTMENT 312, IT was evident no one was home. I looked at Laura's sad eyes. They painted a picture of my disappointment.

"It's Saturday morning. He probably took a walk or maybe had breakfast out." Her hopeful words didn't match her tone.

I nodded. "You're probably right. Let's come back in a couple of hours. That'll give us time to see the Glockenspiel."

Laura and I played off each other's emotions trying to be positive. As hard as it had been to take the steps that brought us to this residence, the thought of leaving without knowing was worse. The hallway back to the elevator seemed longer. We returned to the first floor and walked toward the glass exit doors.

Two elderly ladies in saucer-plate sunglasses and huge straw hats entered in sync holding identical shopping bags. The women wore pink-and-green polka dot scarves tied around their necks.

While Laura tried to keep a straight face, I couldn't help but grin at their quirky attire.

Behind them, a tall man with cropped white hair shuffled through the doors carrying a newspaper. He had dark circles under his eyes. As he got closer, I noticed the deformed knuckle on his right hand — like the knuckle Hans had broken just before the Olympics.

I grabbed Laura's shoulder to stop her from leaving the building and walked after the man. Warmth swirled in my chest. I had connected the dots. Before I even called out to him, "*Mein herr, Bist du* Hans Pepperman?" I knew he was my cousin.

Pausing in front of the elevator, he folded the paper, stuck it under his arm, and slowly turned. "Your German is good for an American. How can I help you?" His accent was definitely German, yet his English was perfect.

Face to face with my family's history, I extended my hand. "I'm Jim Pepperman, Patrick's son."

His tired eyes took on a new light. "Wilhelm's grandson?" He nodded thoughtfully. "How did you recognize me?"

"You look like Grandfather Wilhelm." I wasn't quite ready to explain how I knew about the knuckle.

Still grasping my palm, he laid his other hand on my shoulder. "Even though Patrick was only a young boy when I met him, I can see you have your father's strong jawline. It is a family trait." Grinning, he stepped back, and continued shaking my hand, like he was in as much shock as I was.

My eyes welled up as I turned toward Laura. "Hans, this is my wife, Laura."

He finally let go of my hand and reached to give her a hug. "So glad to meet you." He released her and cupped his fingers over his mouth as though to trap his emotions. He quickly swiped a hand across his eyes and gestured toward the elevator. "Come, we have so much to discuss. So much…"

I pushed the button to open the elevator.

Laura stepped in, then Hans.

I couldn't help but feel the excitement. It was almost electric. This was Hans. Our Hans. It was as though we'd stepped back in time. While he and Laura exchanged small talk on the way to the third floor, I couldn't stop staring at him as I recalled what he'd shared in the journal — the Olympics, the first flight he took on an airplane to Augsburg, his initial encounter with Anna in the elevator at the Bauer Hotel. Having read his memoir made me feel as though I'd been part of his life. This visit was going to be good for all of us. It couldn't be anything less.

The elevator stopped, and Hans walked out first. I swear, his gait was a hundred times better than just a few minutes ago. He unlocked his door, and we followed him inside his apartment.

The impressively upscale modern residence featured floor-to-ceiling windows overlooking the heart of the old city. A large spiral chandelier hung in the center of the room. The furniture, however, was antique in style — heavy oak wall units with doors decorated in green and red floral patterns, armchairs with square legs, bookcases richly carved in design.

A painting on the living room wall caught my attention. It was the front view of a BF 109 fighter plane, the type of plane with the engine Hans had helped design. There was no sign of a swastika—which made sense because Hans had not been a member of the Nazi Party—just the plane emerging from a cloud with a bright blue sky in the background.

He sat us at a double pedestal brown dining set with beautiful high-backed cushioned chairs. The tabletop shone so brightly it reflected everything around it. Laura ran her fingers across the shiny surface as he pulled a chair out for her at the head of the table. "Can I get you something to drink?"

I loved the way his English words resonated with his German accent.

Laura looked at him with bright eyes and a big smile in pure admiration. "No, thank you."

He looked at me.

I shook my head.

He took a chair directly across from me. "Tell me about your father. Through the years I have often thought of him. I was so impressed with his confident manner. I bet he is big like you. Did he ever become a boxer? I remember he had a strong jab for a young boy. He proved it by popping the palm of my hand with his fist. He had eaten a sausage covered in mustard, so I had to wash my hand." His chest moved in an inward laugh.

"He never boxed in amateur competition. But he was a street fighter and taught me how to fight." I leaned back in my chair and hesitated. "He died in an oil field accident when I was seventeen. We lived in Texas at the time."

Hans's lips parted. The look on his face told me he wished he hadn't asked. He nodded but said nothing.

This was a good opportunity to change the subject. "I have something for you." I unzipped the black binder and handed him the journal.

Words couldn't describe his surprise, and I couldn't help but smile as he took the book from me. He opened to the first page as carefully as a man diffusing a bomb. "How did you get this?"

"I was hoping you could tell me. It's a long story, but your journal and trunk ended up in our attic."

He looked at me. "The trunk. Was my Olympic jacket inside?"

I nodded. "Yes."

Hans threw his head back and clutched the journal to his chest. "I would be so happy for you to return it to me. Would you do that, Jim?"

I reached across the table and set my hand on his. "It would be my honor. But I must tell you I read your journal. I hope you don't mind."

"Of course not." He looked at me with a soft, caring smile. "Do you remember Hoermann and Keitel's safe house—the place where my trunk was?"

"Yes."

"I was told the house burned down and everything inside was lost. The Gestapo was looking for me, and I was on the run."

"The house must not have burned, or someone removed the trunk. This is confusing. How did the trunk get to America?" Laura said.

Hans leaned in toward me. "There was a letter inside from your grandfather, and his address was on the envelope. Keitel must have opened the trunk, found the letter, and shipped everything to Wilhelm."

I bit down on my lip and shook my head. "Why would Keitel or anyone ship the trunk to my family? Why didn't he give it back to you?"

Hans slowly shook his head. "I do not know."

I couldn't wait any longer. My heartbeat tripled, and my mouth went dry. "Will you read the last page of your journal and… ?"

"I do not have to read the last page," Hans said. "You want to know who I saw in the film."

CHAPTER 35

July 1999
Munich, Germany

I SCOOTED CLOSER TO LAURA AT HAN'S DINING TABLE.

"You want to know about the person in the film?" Hans's expression intense, he tapped the shiny surface of the table. "This is going to take a while." He pushed out of his chair. "Do you mind if I have some Schnapps? And do you want one?"

"Sure." I really didn't but wanted to be sociable.

He looked at Laura.

She tilted her head. "Maybe a glass of red wine?"

Hans gave her a smile and a salute. "Red wine, it is." He returned with our drinks on a platter, handed me the Schnapps and Laura the wine, and took a sip of his strong liqueur before sitting across from me. The light from the window accented his blue Pepperman eyes and short, silver hair.

This was it. Excitement built from my stomach. All the reading, all the time getting here, I'd thought of very little but the person in the film with Fischer. "So... the film."

Hans put the glass to his lips, paused, and took another sip.

Before he could stall any longer, I reached across the table and "helped" him set his drink down. "Hans, I have to know. Who was it?"

Taking a deep breath in and out, he exhaled the one name I hadn't expected. "Anna."

"What?" I blinked several times, not believing what I'd heard.

Laura's eyes widened, and she sat a little straighter. "Did you just say Anna?"

He glanced away into the living room, then back at me. "Yes, Anna." His voice barely audible, it was as though he didn't even want to speak her name.

"But you wrote in the journal the woman might have been a man in disguise." Laura's voice echoed the tension creeping into my neck and shoulders. "You said you couldn't tell who it was because you couldn't see the face."

"I recognized her hat — a red beret with a black-and-white checked bow." Hans moved his jaw from side to side, his face hardening.

Puzzled by his remark, I shook my head. "Wasn't the film in black-and-white? How could you tell the beret was red?"

"The film was in black-and-white, but the unusual style and checked bow left little doubt it was her. Then I noticed the shape of her calves. It was Anna. I was absolutely sure."

"Oh my gosh." Laura's tone turned sympathetic "It's hard to believe Anna was a Russian spy. You obviously felt something for her. And she loved you."

"There was no love. She used me. Period. She needed me to give up details of the 109 engine."

Leaning forward, Laura set her hand on Hans's. "You must have felt—"

"Betrayed? Shocked? Furious?" He turned his head and did an imaginary spit. "Anna shattered me that day. For a long time, I trusted no one. She had no loyalty to me or her country."

"That sorry." I wanted to curse but held back what I really thought.

Hans pushed on the chair arms, adjusting his position. "I wanted to leave that night and go to her apartment, the rage inside me so uncontrollable I could have killed her. Hoermann and Keitel had to physically restrain me. Hoermann told me to let the Military Intelligence Service deal with her. He left to report what I'd seen on the film. Keitel stayed at the safe house with me."

"And Anna?" I asked.

"The next morning when Hoermann returned, I asked if Anna had been arrested. He said no one could find her. She'd disappeared." Hans rotated his empty glass between his palms, lost in his thoughts as if tormented all over again by his past.

"They never found her?" Laura said.

"Four days later, some hunters discovered her partially nude body in the wooded area north of Augsburg. Her throat had been slashed."

The room went silent. The whisper of a jet engine somewhere above the city of Munich was the only sound.

This was so surreal. I almost wished I hadn't found the journal.

"What about Fischer?" Laura twisted her wedding ring.

"In the film, Anna gave Fischer some folded papers. Hoermann had him arrested." Hans stared at the table and rubbed his eyes. "Espionage cases during the late '30s had speedy trials. Fischer was found guilty and executed for betraying Germany."

Laura scooted her chair closer to the table. "May I have more wine?"

Without speaking, Hans got up from the table and headed back to the kitchen.

Laura followed him with her gaze and stopped at a picture on the wall. "Hans, is that a picture of your wife and daughter?"

"The woman in the picture is my wife, Heidi. The same Heidi in my journal." He disappeared behind a wall.

The world stopped spinning. My chin dropped to the proverbial floor. Laura and I stared at each other for what seemed like minutes until he returned with the wine.

"You married Heidi?" The surprise in Laura's voice pretty much summed up my thoughts as well.

"Heidi was a godsend for me." Hans filled Laura's glass and sat down. "The young girl in the picture is her sister Judy. We never had children. I'm sorry you will miss seeing Heidi. In fact, she is visiting Judy in Dresden."

I glanced at my watch. 11:30. How my world had changed in the span of two hours.

"I had a hard time dealing with Anna and Fischer's deaths. I could not come to grips with them betraying our country. As their friend, Heidi found the situation difficult too. We met after work to comfort each other. And before I knew it, we were spending more time together.

One thing led to another, and we married in September of 1939."

I couldn't imagine what Hans had to deal with. Two close friends who weren't friends at all. They'd used him for their own selfish reasons.

"The war started that same month. I worked overtime at the Bavarian Airworks, and it was good to come home to Heidi at the end of the day. There is an old saying, 'All things work out for the better.' In my case, it could not be truer."

I stretched and extended my legs under the table. "With Anna and Fischer dead, I suppose that was the end of the Russian spying incidents."

Hans gripped his glass so hard his hand shook. "If only what you said were true."

It wasn't his words that chilled my body, it was the way he'd said them.

CHAPTER 36

July 1999
Munich, Germany

Sitting across from Hans, I imagined what his life must have been like. Anna — a spy for the Russian government. I let that sink in. Not only had she betrayed Germany, she'd betrayed Hans by pretending to care for him. She'd used his feelings for her, cutting out his heart in the process, apparently with no remorse. After getting so completely sucked into Hans's story in the journal, I felt like she'd gutted *me*. And her gruesome death only added to the insanity.

"There is more." Hans crossed his arms, angling his body in the chair almost as if he were protecting his heart even now. "The story did not end with Anna."

His contemptuous scowl piqued my interest. I straightened in my chair. "What do you mean?"

He rubbed a hand over his face. "Because she did clerical work for the Gestapo, she was in a perfect position to set me up. She came on to me to get military information, but she also wanted to use me to cover her mistakes."

"Mistakes?" I asked.

"Anna killed Heinrich Adler. He had come by her apartment and tried to rape her. When his body was found near a brothel in Augsburg, I became a suspect. We fought in public the night before. Over Anna. And then the Gestapo found my Olympic lapel pin on the riverbank near his body." He folded a napkin once, then again, before stuffing it into his empty glass. "She stole the pin out of my hotel room and planted it to incriminate me."

I reached across the table. "How did you know Anna killed Adler?"

"I will get to that later." Hans flexed his fingers, tightening them into fists, his disdain for Anna obvious, as if she'd left a stain on his soul he couldn't scrub off.

Laura picked up on it, her shoulders tightening. "You said Adler came by her apartment. If she killed him there, how did she get the body to the brothel?"

"She had help." Hans's tone turned as sharp as cracked Waterford crystal.

Something clicked in my head. I knew who'd helped her. I slammed my open hand on the tabletop. "Fischer."

Hans raised his index finger and ticked it back and forth with the precision of a pendulum on a metronome. "*Nein war es nicht Fischer*." He shook his head. "It was not Fischer."

I looked at Laura, then back at Hans. "Who was it?"

"Hoermann," Hans said. "Hoermann and Anna were partners."

I slapped my hands together, the veins in my neck pounding. That sorry SOB.

Laura's mouth flew open. "Then who killed Anna?"

Hans's face seemed to harden. "After I recognized Anna on the film, Hoermann knew he had to kill her."

"Because once the Gestapo arrested her, she would expose him." Laura said what I had been thinking.

"What about Fischer?" I asked.

Hans's nostrils flared. "Fischer was innocent. Hoermann framed him to make it look like he was working with Anna. He planned to use the film of Anna and Fischer as part of his evidence. He never expected me to recognize her. But Anna's unusual hat, that gave her away."

I rubbed my temple as the twists and turns muddied the water and made Hans's story difficult to follow. "Could you go back to the beginning and help me make sense of what happened?"

"When I first met Hoermann in Stuttgart?" Hans asked.

"Yes, start there, please." My mind needed refreshing.

Shifting in his chair, Hans stared off into space, as if he were trying to keep the past *in* the past. "Messerschmitt had arranged for me to stay and work in Augsburg. I returned to Stuttgart to get my possessions, and Baron asked that I come see him." He slowly tempered his voice until it showed less and less emotion, as though he were building a wall to contain his rage. "Hoermann was in Baron's office smoking a pipe. That was the day he told Baron that Uncle Wilhelm was an American spy and that the Military Intelligence Service would monitor me because of the family ties."

"I remember reading that." Could my grandfather really have been a spy?

"Hoermann was not friendly. I think he had planned to make me a scapegoat as he did Fischer."

"How did you figure all this out?" Laura questioned.

Hans rubbed his hand over the table as if to remove a layer of dust. "I did not figure it out."

Laura leaned in close to Hans's chair, growing as tense as the strings on a tennis racket. "Then who did?"

"Keitel," Hans whispered.

"And how did he know about Hoermann?" Laura gripped the arms of her chair.

The wall Hans was building crumbled a little as a beaten-down look broke through across his face.

It must have been horrible knowing Anna and Hoermann had betrayed him. Not to mention that his true friend, Fischer, had been executed for something he'd had no part in. "I'm sorry, Hans."

The only acknowledgment I got was a stiff nod. "Do you remember when Hoermann, Keitel, and I were in the safe house?"

"Yes," I said.

"And remember when I saw the spy camera in Fischer's chest of drawers and thought it was a pen? Hoermann put it there to incriminate Fischer. He showed me a similar pen in his briefcase and asked me if that was what I had found. That was the first time Keitel suspected him. He wondered why Hoermann would be carrying a spy camera in his briefcase. It did not fit into his job description."

Laura finally gave Hans some breathing room and leaned back in her chair.

"Keitel was a good detective. He went back to the log from the day I was blindsided at the aircraft factory. Hoermann had signed in at 5:25 in the afternoon.

That was not unusual. He would often meet with Messerschmitt at that time of day. When quitting time came, I stayed. The noise I heard that night was Hoermann taking pictures with that pen after he left Messerschmitt's office. I guess he was afraid I would see him, so he knocked me out. For the same reason, he also ran over Fischer when he was unlocking the door to the building about 11:00 p.m."

"I got the impression you weren't too fond of Keitel," I said.

"I was not. But even though he was a Nazi, he was loyal to Germany. He saved me, and I will be forever grateful."

"He saved you?" I asked.

"If it had not been for Keitel, Hoermann's plan to frame me for Anna's murder would have worked."

"I still have questions." Laura had an "oh my" look on her face as she reached over and touched his hand. "The restaurant in Augsburg where you and Anna went, you always sat at the same table. That seemed a little unusual to me."

"Very perceptive of you." Hans gave Laura a humorless, tight-lipped grin. "Hoermann and Anna had that table bugged. Luckily, all the times we had dinner there, I never gave away any secrets about my work. Even though Anna and I were close, I was careful not to talk about the 109 engine, and she rarely asked questions. Heidi, however, asked so many questions you would have thought *she* was the spy." He smiled for the first time since this conversation started.

"How did you know the table was bugged?" I asked.

"Everything came out in Hoermann's trial. When the Gestapo accused him of treason, he became very cooperative."

"I have a few more questions about your journal," Laura said. "Do you mind?"

"It is good for me to talk." Hans looked at both of us. "I am so glad you came. Now, what do you want to ask me?"

"The shortwave radio. Who put it in your hotel room?"

"You are such a delightful person, Laura, and you remember details. A logical thinker. I like that. Hoermann planted that. At the time, he still wanted to frame me as the spy."

"He changed his mind?" Totally into this conversation, Laura couldn't hide her curiosity.

"I have to say… reading the journal I felt like you and Hoermann had become friends. Am I right?"

"Yes, we did become friends." Hans hesitated, as if he were measuring his thoughts. "And I think he did change his mind."

Hans — and his life — fascinated me. What an amazing person. "When did that happen?"

"About the time Hoermann and I went to the Boar's Head Club in Augsburg. He liked the vaudevillian acts and that it was a brothel. The building was old, musty, and smelled of stale beer. Not a place where most people Hoermann worked with would go. He had this phobia about us not being seen together. That was when I told him about being knocked out at the aircraft factory."

Laura shook her head. "But he was the one who knocked you out."

"He played his part. I think he wanted to know how much I remembered about the night, and if I remembered him being there, which I did not." Hans rubbed his chin. "I asked Hoermann about the unusual smell of the tobacco in his pipe. I was beginning to like him then. He was... interesting. Different. I think he was lonely. People were probably put off by his body odor." He paused. "He told me he had picked up the Yello Bole pipe in New York City. The cherry tobacco was his own creation. He had to mix two tobaccos to make the blend."

Several loud police sirens came from the street below. They gave me an eerie feeling, like the police were coming for Hans after all the years. Silly, I know.

Hans sighed. "I may have been his only friend. I could be wrong, but I think that night at the club he decided to frame Fischer instead of me."

Hans pushed back from the table and walked to the window. Hands on his hips, he gazed over the city.

Would he share more about his story? I wished I could read his mind. And I had another important question to ask about Grandfather Wilhelm. Hoermann had accused him of being a spy. The British Spitfire fighter plane had a remarkable engine that was very similar to the 109.

Could Hans have given my grandfather the secret to the engine's performance?

CHAPTER 37

July 1999
Munich, Germany

UNSURE IF HANS KNEW I'D MOVED NEXT TO HIM AT THE window, I briefly set my hand on his shoulder. I couldn't help but wonder if he'd shared his expertise of Germany's prized airplane engine with Grandfather, and if the Americans had passed on that intelligence to the British. "The Spitfire was the British equivalent to the BF 109. Would you agree?"

Behind me, Laura shifted restlessly in her chair.

But clearly lost in thought, Hans continued to look straight ahead. "A remarkable aircraft. The plane's Merlin engine was superb."

"Hans." I cleared my throat. "Was Grandfather Wilhelm an American spy?"

His silence was more deafening than a shotgun blast. Finally, he turned toward me, his face like chiseled stone. "What is your point?"

"If he approached you, would you have shared military secrets about the BF109?"

"Do you think I would betray my country?" His tone hit the edge of hostile. "If I did, I would be no different from Hoermann or Anna."

Had I stepped over the line? How could I have been so stupid? After everything we'd talked about, I'd insulted him. "I didn't mean it that way."

The look he shot me could've stopped a runaway train.

I decided to prod him one more time anyway. But I was careful to keep any accusation from my tone. "I know you love Germany. But I also know you hated the Nazis. To save your country, maybe you helped the Allies?"

All Hans offered was more silence.

I tried a different tactic. "What was it that caused you to hate the Nazi political party?"

His jaw tightened. "You are wrong to assume the Nazi Party was political. It was a dragon that devoured the souls of the German people. A religion with Hitler as the Messiah. A cult. All those who joined were brainwashed into the Nazi ideology—racism, hate, and nationalism that far exceeded the normal pride for one's country." It was impossible not to feel his passion, his disgust for what the Nazis had done to his country. "Any other questions?"

"What happened to you after Anna's death?" Laura asked quietly.

Thank you, Laura, for breaking the tension.

Adjusting his watch, he rubbed his wrist as if the band was too tight and returned to the table.

I followed, reclaiming my seat across from him.

"Schiffter, the Gestapo bureau chief in Augsburg, still blamed me for Adler's death. He also hated me because Hoermann took me out of his custody. And with Anna working for the Gestapo, Schiffter had reason to pursue me again. Knowing I had nothing to do with Adler or Anna's death, Hoermann and Keitel hid me here in Munich."

"Hans." I cocked my head and grinned. "Your life has had more intrigue than a James Patterson novel."

He chuckled, and his shoulders shifted.

"One thing still confuses me. Both the Gestapo and the Military Intelligence Service Hoermann and Keitel worked for were government agencies. I don't get the lack of cooperation between the two."

"Government agencies often do not cooperate." He shrugged. "Character flaws of ego and pride. Both agencies wanted credit. Like apes pounding their chests, shouting, 'Look at me. See what I did.'" Hans closed his eyes and grasped the bridge of his nose.

He looked tired. Bringing up so much tragedy might have been too much. "We're pulling you in every direction."

"We can stop asking questions," Laura offered, unable to hide the disappointment in her voice.

"No." Sighing, he opened his eyes. "But sometimes thinking about the past is hard."

"I'm sorry." I shook my head. "We have no right—"

"But you do. This is part of your family history as much as it is mine. Your generation needs to know about my generation. Please, go ahead and ask."

"How did the Gestapo find out Hoermann killed Anna?" Laura asked.

Hans scratched behind his ear and smiled. "Actually, Keitel tied everything together. The Gestapo found a tobacco pouch with a pipe in it close to Anna's body."

"Hoermann's?" I asked.

Hans nodded. "Keitel saw Schiffter in the lounge at the hotel where I had stayed. When Keitel asked about the investigation of Anna's murder, Schiffter mentioned the pipe but said he was unable to tie it to anyone. Keitel filled Schiffter in about Hoermann's smoking habits. When Hoermann and Keitel came to see me in Munich, Keitel slipped the pouch with the pipe on a side table. Hoermann saw the pouch and said, 'Ah, so this is where I left it.' At this point, Keitel arrested him. The shocked look on Hoermann's face left no doubt he had been caught. He did not even put up a fight."

"The SOB got his." I made a fist and pounded my palm. *Pow! Pow!* "The perfect payback."

"I had not thought about it, but it was the perfect payback." Hans grinned. "That is an excellent observation. Bravo. Good point."

"So, Keitel turned Hoermann over to the Gestapo, and he was tried for treason and murder?" Laura cupped her hands over her mouth. I couldn't see her smile, but her eyes gave it away.

"The same judge who had presided over Fischer's trial also presided over Hoermann's. Quite a twist of fate, would you not say?" Hans's deep baritone laugh told me he did get retribution. He glanced at his watch. "I told Heidi I would call her, and it is almost 4:00. Do you mind?"

"No, of course not," I said.

"We need to get back to the hotel." Laura pushed out of her chair. "We promised our boys we'd call them."

Hans and I stood and shook hands.

He gave Laura a one-arm squeeze around the shoulder. "I want to hear about your boys tomorrow."

"Yes, we'll take you to lunch." I wished we could spend the rest of the summer in Munich. There was so much more I wanted to know about Hans. "We have one more day here, and we'd love to spend it with you."

"*Wunderbar. Wunderbar.*" His voice boomed with excitement.

Laura and I spent the rest of the afternoon enjoying the sites of the old German city and rehashing our conversation with Hans. I couldn't wait to tell him about our boys.

The next day we had an early breakfast and walked around the Marienplatz until time to go back to Hans's apartment. At 11:45, I knocked on his door.

No answer.

I knocked again.

The lady directly across the hall opened her door. Frail with rounded shoulders and spindly legs, she was barely able to walk. "Are you Hans's *die familie*?" she asked.

"Yes, my cousin." I looked at the lady, at Laura, then back at the lady. I didn't have a good feeling about what she was going to say.

"Hans was called away to Dresden." She hesitated. "His wife Heidi had emergency surgery. But he told me she would be fine and not to worry. He asked me to give you this." As she extended her hand, her gnarled fingers shook.

I took the cream-colored envelope from her and half bowed to show respect. "*Dunke schoen.*"

She smiled and turned back toward her apartment, her shuffled steps small and labored.

I felt a tug to my heart. Our first meeting with Hans shouldn't end this way.

Laura's face echoed my feelings.

We went back to the elevator and pushed the button to the first floor. We didn't talk as we exited the building and started back to the hotel.

Laura touched my arm as we passed a *biergarten*. "Let's have a drink and read what's in the envelope."

We sat at an outdoor table. I opened the envelope and pulled out the cream-colored paper.

The bold penmanship was almost as legible as the journal entries sixty-two years ago. "You do the honors." I handed the note to Laura.

She leaned close to me. "Jim, it was such a joy to meet you and Laura," she read softly. "Over sixty years have passed since I met your father Patrick at the Olympics. He impressed me with his strong physical features and confident demeanor. Even as a young boy, he was imposing. Seeing you reminds me of him. I look forward to meeting your sons. I am sure the Pepperman genes are present in each of them."

I laughed.

Laura smiled and continued reading. "Heidi, the joy of my life, wishes she could have met you. You would like her. She never meets a stranger and loves being with family. I want you to know I did meet up with your Grandfather Wilhelm after the Olympics. He was a good, proud American fighting for his country. A true patriot. Have a safe trip home. Hans."

She pushed the note toward me, and I leaned back in my chair.

I wished I could've asked Hans when he met up with Grandfather. Was it before the war started in 1939? Or was it after? And how many times did they meet? Straightening in my chair, I angled toward Laura. "When we get home, I'm going to research the life of Grandfather Wilhelm and find out everything about him."

Laura brushed her hand across her face. A pesky fly wouldn't leave her alone. "That sounds interesting. But why?"

"In the note" —I jabbed my finger at the piece of paper —"it says Hans and Grandfather met up after the Olympics. Hans never said he gave up German secrets, but he never said he didn't. So... had he and Grandfather both been spies?"

Laura exhaled and shook her head. "There may be a reason Hans didn't tell you about their relationship."

"But the note reeks with suspicion."

"I don't know why he didn't tell us," Laura said. "That's his business. Maybe he was sparing us details that would throw an entirely different light on himself and your grandfather. In time, Hans may tell you the whole story, but now he's not willing. Just let it go." She reassured me with a smile.

I folded the note, put it in my pocket, and kissed Laura on the cheek. "Let's go home."

CONNECT WITH BILL

The best thing about writing is hearing from my readers and establishing relationships.

Get a FREE ebook! Join my NEWSLETTER for book information, new releases, and special deals. Sign up on the bottom of the homepage of my website at BillBriscoe.com.

FIND ME ONLINE

Website: BillBriscoe.com
Contact Form: BillBriscoe.com/contact
Email: BillBriscoe@BillBriscoe.com
X (Twitter): BILLDBriscoe
Facebook Author Page: billbriscoe
Instagram: billbriscoebooks

ABOUT THE AUTHOR

Read more at billbriscoe.com

Bill Briscoe grew up in the best part of the Texas pan-handle — in an oil and gas refinery town called Phillips. With a population of 4,000, most people were of the same socioeconomic level, company-owned homes had white asbestos siding and green composition roofs, and almost everyone drove Fords or Chevys.

After graduating with a master's degree in educa-tion, Bill spent most of his career working for a major insurance company as an agency manager and consul-tant. About five years before retirement, he told his wife he wanted to write a novel based on an idea that had been simmering in his head for ten years. That book is *Pepperman's Promise*, the prequel to *The Pepperman Mystery* Series.

When he's not writing, Bill enjoys visiting sports venues across the country. He's attended baseball games in Wrigley Field (Chicago), Camden Yards (Baltimore), St. Louis, and Arlington as well as college football at Baylor, University of Texas, Texas Tech, Ole Miss, and The University of Oklahoma. One especially memorable trip was to South Bend, Indiana, to watch Notre Dame play football. Bill married his wife, Liz, in 1969. They have two daughters, Blythe and Brook, and two grand-children, Chloe and Foster.

The Pepperman Mystery Series
Pepperman's Promise (Prequel)
Perplexity (Book One)
Panic Point (Book Two)
Perfect Payback (Book Three)
Puzzle Piece (Book Four)

You can find all Bill's books at BillBriscoe.com/books

A WORD FROM THE AUTHOR

Thank you for reading *Perfect Playback*. You can help others find it by recommending it or leaving a review. Reviews don't have to be long or go into detail. Thanks in advance for your time.

If you enjoyed this book, check out *The Pepperman Mystery* Series in its entirety.

Pepperman's Promise (Prequel). Not a mystery but contemporary fiction, this book lays the groundwork for the characters in the series and follows a young Jim Pepperman through his twentieth high school reunion as he tries to fulfill an impossible promise he made to his dad.

Perplexity (Book One). Jim must face a mistake from his past that threatens to derail his future.

Panic Point (Book Two). After Earl's bride vanishes in the Smoky Mountains on their honeymoon, the former Navy SEAL puts his life on the line to find her.

Perfect Payback (Book Three). When Jim and his wife Laura find a musty German Olympic jacket and an old journal in their attic, they stumble onto a gripping pre-World War II story of a cousin Jim knew nothing about.

Puzzle Piece (Book Four). A death thirty-five years ago. One old bloodstained shirt. Can it hold a clue to prove the long-ago death was murder?

ACKNOWLEDGEMENTS

I want to thank Jodi Thomas, New York Times Best Selling Author, for her encouragement. She always has time for me and makes me feel I can accomplish my dream of becoming a writer. Her influence has started the careers of many successful authors. Exceptional lady.

A special thanks to Morgan Hysinger and Melody Hysinger. You two have been a blessing for sure. I can never repay you for being so generous with your advice on this writing journey.

I would also like to thank the following people who helped bring this book to reality:

Editor: Lori Freeland

Cover and Video Artist: Fiona Jayde, Fiona Jayde Media

Formatting: Tamara Cribley, The Deliberate Page

Website and Computer Support: Michael Gaines

Beta Readers: Sharyn Leiter, Mike Leiter, George Brownlee

Proofreading Team: Brenda Brownlee, Jeff Stenberg, Ora Mae Brownlee, Marjo van Patten